IS IT SUICIDE OR MURDER?

IS IT SUICIDE OR MURDER?

Kevin M. Weeks

With Book Cover Artwork by
Paul Mitchell

Library of Congress Control Number:		2006905186
ISBN 10:	Hardcover	1-4257-1105-7
	Softcover	1-4257-1104-9
ISBN 13:	Hardcover	978-1-4257-1105-4
	Softcover	978-1-4257-1104-7

1. Jackson, Teco (Fictitious character)—Fiction. 2. Strictly Business (SB)—Fiction. 3. Young Black Mafia—Fiction. 3. Theft, Crimes, Murders, Illegal drugs and activities—Fiction. 4. Law Enforcement Officers—Fiction. 5. Philadelphia (PA)—Fiction. 6. Conshohocken (PA)—Fiction. 7. Neighborhood—Fiction. 6. Washington (D.C.)—Fiction. I. Title.

This book was printed in the United States of America.

To order additional copies of this book, contact:
Xlibris Corporation
1-888-795-4274
www.Xlibris.com
Orders@Xlibris.com
33053

DEDICATION

To Mercedes Weeks, Chanell Weeks, and Kevin M. Weeks, Jr.,

Sunshine,

and Marcelus Griffen (Polo) R.I.P.

Author's Notes

Urban Adult Fiction

Parental Advisory: Contains Adult Situations, Explicit Language, Drug Use, and Strong Sexual Content

SPECIAL ACKNOWLEDGEMENTS

I want to first thank *God* for giving me the gift to write. *René*, I want to thank you for believing in me and giving me that peace of being "in the gap." 1-4-3. *Brandon Lewis*, I thank you for being that mortar which brought René and me together. *Akia Bostic*, I will always take time to hear you out. We seem to have been on the same page with *The Street Life Series* concept. *Signe Adderley*, Mom, I know you thought that I would never put this book out. You are the world's greatest mother. I love you. To my siblings: *Tony*, I thank you for being hard on me, when we were younger. I've learned a lot from you, which will always stay with me. *Trezonna*, I want to thank you for those times when I needed you and you came to big brother's side. *Denise*, I want you to know that you have been my number one artist. You stay focused. To my Dad, *Anthony Weeks*, I thank you for your wise sayings that I reflect upon today for guidance. RIP Dad. *Grandmom Hazel Blackwell*, I thank you for your prayers when it seemed as though no one had been praying. I love you. *Edwina Loftlin*, cuz, I thank you for reaching out to provide me with your love. I want to give a special thank you to *Retired SGM Clyde Durden*. I must say that you have been a huge rock in my life; and I can see why you've never lost a soldier; and you never will. I didn't understand the impact of a mentor until I worked for you. Thank you and I'll always apply "hindsight, insight, and foresight" into my life. To *Mrs. Saundra Hood*, you gave me the first opportunity to demonstrate my professional skills as a motivational speaker in order to inspire others. With that said, thank you. *Mr. George Gaye*, I thank you for being that father figure when I lived the street life. You'll always be remembered. *George Gaye, Jr. and Rodney Gaye*, I thank you both for the time when we ran the streets and had to grind to get to the other side of the bridge. To all my nieces, nephews, aunts, uncles, and cousins, here it is in the raw form and many to follow, I thank you all for your strong support. Thank you.

To all those brothers, who put up with me when I was working on this project in Cobb County Georgia ADC A-4, ASMP, & DSP, to Lil "D", Focus, Willie D., Bert, Montrel, J Roxx, Reece, and to all other aspiring authors, I thank you all for taking the time to support my first work. Thank you. To those who looked at me as if I were crazy while God was blessing me to write this novel and to those who turned their backs on me during a pivotal point when I needed them the most, I have nothing but love for you all. Thanks to the United States Postal Service for delivering my manuscript safely.

A king will arise in his time. Thank you all. See you on the freedom side.

CHAPTER 1

In the fall of 1988, Teco Jackson was known as a troublemaker in West Philly. His hood was 58th and Baltimore Avenue. On this cool breezy night, Teco walked up 52nd Street headed towards 60th and Market looking for an easy car to steal. To the thugs in the hood, this type of car was known as a Johnny. As Teco focused on the cars parked on the street, the thought crossed his mind that he also needed a place to sleep for the night. It wasn't a secret that Teco didn't have a permanent place to live. He roamed all over Philly at times in search of somewhere safe to rest. When things were really tight, Teco slept in some of the Johnnies he stole.

As Teco passed by the 52nd and Market Street L line subway station, he could hear the train leaving. The iron wheels made a loud screeching noise, which caused goose bumps to appear on his masculine arms. At 1:30 in the morning, the street lights made it possible to see in dark doorways. The streets had been somewhat empty. There were a couple of people in front of Kelly's Bar as well as a few fiendish crackheads chasing that White Ghost and willing to do anything to find him.

A female crackhead saw Teco approaching. She had never observed a young man so debonair until she saw this tall, fine ass, brother walking her way. With a toothpick in his mouth, Teco had the sexiest gangster stride imaginable. The diamond earring in his left ear sparkled under the street lights. She envisioned being cheek to cheek against his dark chocolate face, which was smooth as cocoa butter. The tiny scar under his right eye gave him a rugged look which was most attractive. Looking at his broad shoulders and his rock hard shape caused her nipples to respond. The closer he got to her, she noticed him rubbing his black wavy hair and licking his full-sized lips.

The female crackhead walked up to Teco and asked, "Hey, you workin'?"

Teco looked at her and asked, "Yeah, what do you need?"

She was thinking, *"I need a fine lookin' man like you to take me to yo crib and gimme some."* She smelled a subtle hint of Drakkar Noir cologne on his neck. This made her wish she could turn back the clock to a time when men noticed her inner and outer beauty. So instead she replied, "I need a twenty piece."

"Gimme the money; and I'll be back," said Teco.

"Hell no, I don't know you like that."

"Fuck you then, you crackhead."

Teco walked away, but deep inside he knew he needed the money to catch the train to 60th and Market Street. This was where he would get his cars, in the vicinity of Sears department store. If he didn't get the cash, he would have to walk seven long blocks and timing was a major factor. He already had another plan in motion on how he could get the money; and there she was right in front of him. Before he could speak, Ghost Chaser grabbed him on his large biceps and asked, "Okay here's the dough. Is it some good stuff?"

"Yeah, it's straight butta, just wait right here," said Teco.

She watched him like a night hawk as he dug in the rubbish pile and pulled out a small brown paper bag. He flagged her over to him. She came closer; and he gave her a plastic octagon shaped tube, which had some little rocks inside. Unfortunately, she didn't know that he had just sold her a ball of wax. Right after he made the deal, he went up the street towards the train station entrance. While he was going up the steps, he could hear Ghost Chaser yelling, "Hey you black ass fake po hustler, gimme back my muthafuckin' money. This shit ain't real!"

When Teco heard her, he exclaimed, "Oh Shit!" Teco started running faster up the stairs. Once he paid to get on the train, he knew that he would be safe. Upon stepping onto the platform, he went to find a seat. Teco's very hard breathing brought even more attention to him; and he realized that five people were staring him down. When the train came, it was 2:30am which was about the right time for Teco to steal a car from the Sears employee parking lot.

As Teco came to his stop, the conductor shouted over the loud speaker with a commanding voice, "Last stop 60th Street Station!" When Teco stood up, he looked out the window. From that side, he became excited about all the cars that were below. He was thinking of nothing but dollars. He started patting his side to be sure the screwdriver was still in place. Then he felt his back pocket and checked for the spark plug. He knew this would be an easy job. They all were easy for Teco.

As he ascended from the L line train station, he looked all around to see if anybody would witness him jumping the fence. He was standing in a very dark doorway of a small store, so no one could notice him. The street lights had been out, like several of the street lights in West Philly. He stood there for ten minutes and then started to move. Suddenly, he stopped because he heard some footsteps. As he lay low, two dudes came walking past drinking Olde English 800, which Teco called 8 Ball. They never noticed Teco standing in the cut of the store.

When the streets seemed clear, Teco made his move. He slid his back against the wall until he came to the six foot fence. He put the screwdriver through the diamond hole and looked one more time behind him. He placed his left hand on the wire, then his right hand gripping tightly. Teco was trying his best not to make any noise, because the parking lot had a security guard shed. Unaware if anybody was in there, he stood still until he felt that the coast was clear. With one hard pull, he was over the fence. Once he hit the ground, Teco didn't move. He looked around and rose up to make his way past the security booth. Seeing that no one was in there put Teco at ease. As he walked around the parking lot looking for a good car, he came to an abrupt stop, breaking in his tracks.

"Damn, what was that noise?" He was crouched down low to the ground like a black alley cat ready to pounce. As he scanned to his far right, he saw a female with a Sears vest on walking to her car. *"That chick scared the hell out of me."* As she got into her car, he watched as she drove away. She never noticed him hunched between two cars next to her.

Teco came up next to a 1987 Chrysler Lebaron, which was white with a blue soft top. He reached in his back pocket and pulled out the spark plug. He laid it on the ground. With the handle of the screwdriver, he struck the spark plug. Bam! Bam! The spark plug broke into little pieces. Teco picked up one little piece and threw it at the small back window on the driver's side, causing glass to shatter into little pieces. This made a real faint sound as the glass hit the ground. Teco cleared the rest of the back window with the handle of the screwdriver. After doing that, he reached in the car to open the back door. There was a soft click as the door unlocked. He pulled the door handle, making sure to move fast and swift without the interior lights coming on. Once inside, he climbed to the front and was ready to jam the screwdriver in the steering column; but for some odd reason, he had an intuitive vibe. He didn't know why; but he reached and opened the glove compartment. There appeared a fake blue Gucci purse.

Teco pulled out the purse and opened it. Not expecting to find anything but cosmetics, his eyes opened wide. There it was and he couldn't believe it. He pulled out the key to the car. He put the key in the ignition and turned it over. Though there was a brief pause, the car started right up off the jump.

"Damn, you can't get no betta than this."

He put the car in reverse to pull out of the parking spot. As he came to the entrance of the parking lot, Teco looked both ways and drove off. He made a left turn going toward Cobbs Creek Parkway. As he looked in the rear-view mirror, he noticed that a police patty wagon was coming up behind him. When Teco came to Cobbs Creek Parkway, he put on his right signal blinker. The police seemed to be following Teco.

"Shit, I just got this chumpie!"

There was an Exxon coming up on his left side. So he pulled to the far left center lane and slowed down to turn into the gas station. The police was right behind him. Teco drove up to Pump #4. He watched the patty wagon park on the side of the gas station building.

"What in hell does he want?"

Teco got out of the car, walked inside the gas station, and at the same time wondered if he should run. He put $10 on pump #4 and bought a pack of Bubble Yum. On his way out, he heard a deep authoritative voice say, "Sir, may I speak with you?" Teco turned his head; and there stood a white cop who was tall enough to play in the NBA.

"Yeah, wassup?" asked Teco, who was looking for a path in case he had to make a run for it.

"Can you tell me where you are coming from?" asked the cop.

"I was comin' from Sears. I just dropped off my girl for work. Why are you askin'?"

"Because we don't find many people driving around this part of West Philly 3 in the morning with a broken window."

Teco was accustomed to being questioned. *"I need to start walkin' as if I have the right to be out this late."* Teco raised his left eyebrow and replied to the cop, "Don't worry. I'll get the window fixed."

As he went back to the car he pulled off the gas cap, filled the car up with gas, and continued to keep his eyes on the police. After he finished pumping the gas, he got into the car and drove away. He put his hand on his chest to feel how fast his heart was beating. *"That shit was close as hell."*

He rode for about ten minutes before he turned on the radio. When he did, the station was tuned to Power 99 FM. As the speakers got louder, he turned the volume up to hear Run DMC playing, "My Adidas!" Teco rocked his head and jammed with the rap song. This was his victory dance. The only thing going through his big head was dollar signs for this Johnny.

As he passed Anderson Middle School, he saw the library. When the light changed, he approached 58th and Baltimore Avenue. This is where Teco grew up. He looked at the street corner; and there stood five guys. Three of them were his homies; and the other two he didn't know. He could tell that they all were smoking weed, so he slowed down. Then he came to a complete stop.

"Whatz up, Cowboy, Vernon, and Torry?" asked Teco.

"Yo, whatz up wit you Teco? Where did you get this ride?" asked Cowboy.

"You know how I do it. I get nothin' but the best."

He then pulled into the Burger King parking lot, which was right across the street from his homies. He ran over to them and gave them some dap as they passed him the blunt. When he was about to leave, Stacy Calloway showed up on the block. She walked up to Teco, gave him a big hug, and asked, "Hey Teecoo, what you been up to tonight or shall I say this morning?"

"I see you checkin' up on me. Why yo young ass out this early in the mornin' anyway? Yo momma know you out here?" asked Teco teasingly.

"Pleez, you just turned 21 ya own damn self," said Stacy as she playfully hit Teco on his upper arm.

"WOooo, you know she right dawg," said Vernon. Then they all laughed.

Stacy turned to Teco and said, "Meet me at my crib in ten minutes."

Teco really liked Stacy, because he had a thing for short women. Her skin was the color of dark brown sugar; and she had long black hair, which glistened in the lights on the streets. As she walked, her breast, bow legs, and ass came at you, like a tropical dish of fruit, cock-, and a thick -tale. Stacy and Teco attended Shaw Middle School back in the day when he was in eighth grade and she was in the seventh. There was this one time that Teco had to fight these dudes from 54th Street for her. Teco knew that she was from his block, because he had seen her at the local Recreation Center named Sharwood on Cedar Avenue. They had never been formally introduced, but he knew he had to protect her. Soon, they had become real close friends, walking to and from school together.

Stacy's best friends told her that Teco was sleeping around. She actually knew they were right. Her mother didn't like Teco either and warned her that he was no good. For some unknown reason, Stacy believed in Teco and always let him come back into her life. She was looking forward to a positive response from him.

Teco looked at her and said, "Word, I'll be there." Then he kissed her on the forehead.

That next morning as Teco opened his eyes, he saw his beautiful Stacy standing in the basement doorway in a Mickey Mouse t-shirt and pink panties. "Hey Baby," said Stacy.

"Wassup sexy? Come ova here and gimme some of that good kitty kat." He was horny all over again.

"Damn, you greedy. Last night you tried to break my back."

"You're the one who told me to break you off proper." He said with a smirk on his face.

"You knew what I meant. All I have for you is breakfast and a kiss. My kitty kat is sore." Her eyes squinted as she patted herself. Then she gave him an enticing wink.

"My fault, you know that I haven't had any of that good kitty kat in a while. I had to let you know I was in there."

She gave Teco an impatient look and said, "Yeah, yeah, whateva, just hurry up and get dressed before my mom comes down here." Stacy didn't want to hear her mom's sermon about Teco today.

Teco got up out of Stacy's bed and walked to the basement bathroom. He took a nice cold shower. As he was drying off, he thought of the car he had last night and exclaimed, "Shit!" He rushed out of the bathroom to find his clothes, so he could make a mad dash. "Stacy, I need to jet!"

"See Teco, all you do is hit and run."

"No, it's not like that, I got a Johnny at Burger King."

"You know that shit is gone by now."

"No, not this one, I got keys to this ride."

As Teco was talking to Stacy, he was also getting dressed. Teco walked towards the basement door to leave. He glanced back and saw that Stacy was sitting on the bed with her arms crossed. Without giving her a kiss, Teco dipped out.

CHAPTER 2

While walking up the block, he could see the car from Cookies, the neighborhood corner store. He looked around for a few minutes to see if any police had the car on watch; and there were none. He walked to the car, as if he had the right to drive it, opened the door, got in, and drove away.

While sitting at a red light, he went through the purse and found $60, which he decided to use to repair the broken car window. He headed to the Skylite Glass Shop, where they fixed it for $25. Within 30 minutes, the window was replaced. Skylite even vacuumed up the glass for him. Now, all he had left to do was to get the car washed.

Down the street from Skylite was Cobbs Creek Car Wash, where Teco took the car to be cleaned. While he waited, he saw this female that reminded him of one of his old girlfriends. *"That looks like Lynn."* He got up to see; but by the time he reached the glass door, she was gone. So, he walked outside; and just that quickly, there she was right in his face. It wasn't Lynn; however, he had to say something. "Excuse me, how are you doin'?" Teco asked in a sexy voice.

"I'm doing fine." She said softly.

"Look, my name is Teco."

She saw where he was going with this and decided to play along with him. "So, wassup wit you?" she asked.

"Nothin', just chillin'. So, what's yo name?"

"Tina B," said Tina Campbell, who was short with vibrant Indian-like hair. Her big bodacious round ass rocked from side to side when she strolled down any street. Her hips reminded Teco of the curves, bends, and turns in Belmont Plateau. Her breast sure set her figure off.

The first thing she noticed was Teco's brilliant smile. As he spoke to Tina, she observed that Teco's hand gestures were inviting and that she wanted to reach out and touch him. His facial expressions were animated during their conversation. She found herself laughing at Teco's simple comments as well as his player questions. Tina couldn't understand how he captivated her attention in such a small amount of time. For sure, Teco reminded her of black ice, which is real slick and causes your car to run off the road on a frozen winter's night.

"What does the 'B' stand for?" asked Teco.

"You don't even want to know."

"Believe me, I want to know. I've heard it all."

"Well the guys in my hood say I have a lot of booty; so they call me big butt Tina, Tina B. for short."

"I would have to agree wit them, respectfully, of course." As he looked around her body to see the rest of her, he continued to say, "You do have some beef behind you." Then Teco realized what he had said to Tina. *"Damn, I didn't mean to say that out loud."*

"Excuse you?" Tina asked as she rolled her eyes at him. Yet, she thought Teco had a certain charm that made her want to see him again.

She was tight looking, as Teco looked her up and down wanting to have her right there. He refocused and asked, "Well look, I need to take care of some business. Do you think we can get together later?"

"You can take my number. We will talk later, if you find the time." Tina said sarcastically. She wrote her digits down on a piece of paper. Just as she was giving him the paper, the car wash employee drove Teco's Johnny to the front; and it was shining like new.

"Nice car." Tina B. said impressed.

"Thanks, I'll give you a call fo sho."

As he drove off, he was thinking of whom he could visit on this side of town. Teco loved to impress the women. Men used various names for a woman in the hood, like ho, hoodrat, and hoochie to name a few. If Teco ever heard a dude calling his sisters these names, he would knock them out. Now calling the girls skimmies was more like it. So, he headed to Mt. Airy to show these skimmies his new ride, as if he were the owner. He was scheming about something to get into.

Teco and his family once lived in Mt. Airy, on the 8300 block of Williams Avenue. Teco had two younger sisters named Lenise Jackson, whom everyone called Niecee, and Keisha Jackson, whom Teco called Kee. Both sisters were absolutely knock-out gorgeous. Good looks ran through the Jackson family genes.

After reaching Mt. Airy, he had to see if his homey, Bernard Gordon, a.k.a. Fatboy, was home. Fatboy met Teco through Niecee. Fatboy was tall with just enough court game not to be the last player picked for street basketball. His athletic body drove the ladies wild. Fatboy's sandy brown hair color complimented his Mandingo skin tone. Even though Fatboy was younger than Teco, they had lots in common.

When Niecee had problems at school with some of the guys, Teco would go to the school to put those pussies in check about his sister. One day Niecee was complaining about this dude messing with her all the time. A few days later when Niecee and Teco were walking to the park, Teco rocked this same dude at the baseball field for just saying Niecee's name. There was a huge crowd of onlookers. One of the guys in the crowd cheering was Fatboy. Niecee introduced them when things calmed down. Fatboy gave Teco props for taking up for Niecee. From that moment on, Fatboy and Teco had become friends and rode together.

Teco couldn't wait to show Fatboy his Johnny. Fatboy lived on the 7800 block of Fayett Avenue. Teco parked the car and knocked on the door. Fatboy's sister, Francene, came to the door. "Hey Teco, wassup?"

"Nothin', just chillin'. Where is Fatboy?"

"He's downstairs. Come on in." When Teco stepped in the house, he sat down on the sofa. Francene called to her brother at the top of her voice, "Fatboy! Teco's up here for you!"

Fatboy came up from the basement looking high as hell and only wearing shorts. "Yo Teco, what's the deal?" asked Fatboy.

"You tell me, lookin' like you from China."

"Come downstairs and say hello to Mary Jane."

Once they were in the basement, Teco pulled out the key to the car and said, "Yeah boy, it's on tonight. Yo, get dressed and let's ride to the Ivy Hill Bar."

Once they got into the car, Fatboy fired up another bud. They were jamming to Power 99 FM on the way over. "Yo Teco, where did you get this Johnny?"

"From West Philly by Sears."

"Man I know we can pull some skimmies in this fly ass ride. When can I drive this bad boy?"

"Man you high. Just chill and enjoy the hype, because it'll never last long." Teco rarely let anyone, high or not, drive his cars. For Teco to be in the passenger's seat gave him an uncomfortable feeling. So, he was very evasive to Fatboy's desire to drive.

As soon as they drove up to the front door, these two skimmies were trying to flag them down as if they knew Teco and Fatboy. Teco was hoping to see these sexy ladies inside. The parking lot was full, which meant that the bar was packed. They had to park at the Thriftway Supermarket across the street.

It cost $3 to get into the bar; and just as they thought, the place was packed. In the back of the bar, you could see those Young Black Mafia (YBM) boys with women all around them. As Teco moved more closely, his eye's squinted to get a better visual. "What the fuck my sister doin' wit those dope boyz?"

"I don't know, but she sure looks good." Fatboy said with a smirk on his face. Teco gave Fatboy a cold look.

"Fatboy, I'll be right back." Teco started walking towards the table. As he got closer, two guys stood up with their hands in their jackets, as if they were getting ready to pull out some heat. Teco knew they were carrying, but he didn't give a fuck about anything when it came to his family. He put his hands up. "Yo, just chill. I need to talk to my sista, Kee."

Some dude in the back asked, "Who the hell are you?"

"I'm Teco, who you?" Teco looked as if the dude in the back should be bowing down to him. The dude said something to his boys and they sat down. Another dude said something to Teco's sister. Kee stepped down from the platform to meet her brother and asked, "Boy, what you want?"

"What are you doin' wit them YBM boyz?"

"See there you go mindin' my business and actin' like you my father."

"Girl stop trippin'. Let's dance."

"I'm not dancin' wit you. You my brutha." She snapped her head and turned to walk away from Teco.

Fatboy walked over to Teco. "Yo, what was that 'bout?"

"Nothin', she's just trippin' thinkin' she's all cute and fly. Anyway Fatboy, what do these skimmies look like up in here?"

"Come ova here and see this fine ass skimmie wit a fly hair-do."

As they walked through the crowd to get a good visual, Teco smiled. "Man, I know her, that's Kim. She works at the pizza joint up the street," said Teco.

"Stop frontin'. You don't know her," said Fatboy.

"Okay homey, check this. If I prove you wrong, you buy the first round of drinks."

"If it's like that then, dance wit her, Mr. Don Juan."

"Just like the original Don Juan, a masterful seducer. Take note of the moves." Teco said as he did a smooth spin and eased into his pimp walk.

Teco knew that he was boss with the women. Even with his very rugged look, Teco is still handsome all the same. He made his way to the ladies' table. Kim's back was turned to him; so he reached out and tapped her on her right shoulder. "Yo, wassup Kim?"

She turned around not knowing who was interrupting her conversation. Nonchalantly she asked, "Hey Teco, wassup?"

"Nothin', just chillin'. And you?"

"Just chillin' wit my girls. I haven't seen you since—"

"Since what, the last time I beat you on the dance floor?"

Kim got up, put her hands on her hips with the "sista girl" headshake and said, "Now you know you never beat me at nothin'."

"Oh really? That must have been someone else, right?"

"Well, let's see if yo ass is ready to get loose tonight. I've got some new moves for you."

As Teco and Kim started walking towards the dance floor, Teco looked at Fatboy. Fatboy threw up two fingers acknowledging that drinks were on him. Then Fatboy stood at the bar talking to some skimmies, as Rob Base's song "It Takes Two" blared from the speakers.

Teco and Fatboy had a lot of fun dancing and playing the women. The night was getting late; and the bar was thinning out. "Yo, I'm ready to vamp. I'll meet you at the car. I need to find my sista," said Teco.

Teco went to the table where the YBM boys were seated; however, the group had left. He ran outside to see if he could catch her. As soon as he reached outside, his eyes focused on this black limousine and blue Volkswagen Jetta. He saw his sister walking towards the limo. "Hey Kee!" Teco shouted, "I need to talk to you!" She turned around at her brother's voice and headed in his direction.

"What do you want Teco?" She was really getting tired of him.

"Hey sis, can you hook a brutha up wit some bread?"

"Boy, I don't have any money."

"See how you do me. Just gimme $30."

"Boy here and you betta stop smokin' that weed."

"Girl don't front on me out here. Wassup wit those gangsta boyz you wit?" As she gave him the money, she explained that they were from the YBM and Strictly Business (SB) Crew; and they had big bucks.

"Yo, can you put me down or what? You know I'm game to get paid," said Teco.

"Teco, these boyz don't play. They are big time money makers."

"Do they buy flipped cars?"

"Boy everything they drive is legal. What you can do is come to their crib. I'll give you some of their fly gear. They got clothes up the ying-yang. Come ova there tomorrow when everybody is gone."

"So where do they stay?"

"On the 7800 block of Williams Avenue at the last house on the left wit the red door. Come at 4pm."

When Kee got into the limo, the guy she was with named Leon Wilson, a.k.a. Cap, looked at her and asked, "Wassup with yo brutha?"

"Nothin', he just beggin' me for money as usual," said Kee.

"I was just wonderin' 'cause he seems like he's down for whateva," said Cap.

"No, he ain't no hustler. He steals cars." Kee laughed.

"Oh yeah, he may be useful later," said Cap.

"Look, don't put my brutha down wit no bullshit."

"Baby come on, you know that I wouldn't do him like that," said Cap, who was short with a slender build. Cap walked with a limp because of a gun shot injury; however, he was good at the street game. He lacked two essential qualities to run a crew, which were leadership skills and sex appeal. But this didn't matter to the SB Crew, because Cap's heart was as big as Philly. Kee didn't know that Cap had no rank or pull at SB or YBM. He was just a runner and played the big boy part.

Fatboy and Teco got in the car and drove off. "Yo, that girl you were dancin' wit was bad. Why didn't you pull up on that skimmie?" asked Fatboy.

"Man, you know I can have that anytime I want."

"Yeah that's what your mouth says." Fatboy said in a laughing manner.

"You said it yo'self. I am Mr. Don Juan." Teco replied as he put a toothpick in his mouth. They both laughed and drove off into the street life.

CHAPTER 3

The next morning, Teco woke up and said, "Fatboy, thanks for lettin' me stay at yo crib last night."

"Man, keep it down. You know how my dad is," said Fatboy.

Teco fell back asleep, until Fatboy's dad came into the basement and tapped Teco on the forehead. "What the hell are you doin' here?" asked Mr. G.

Teco was trying to gain his focus on who woke him up. Once he realized it was Mr. G., he quickly offered an explanation. "I was drinkin' last night and couldn't drive," said Teco.

"Are you drunk now?" asked Mr. G.

"No, not really. Why? Wassup?"

"Well get up and help me wit my car."

Teco could never understand why Mr. G. only asked him to help with the chores. Fatboy never assisted his dad with anything. Teco was the one who had to listen to Mr. G. philosophize about life. Teco got up and helped Mr. G. with his car, which took 3 hours to finish.

After that was done, Teco walked to his Johnny and made sure all was well. He looked at his watch and saw that it was almost time to go to see his sister, Kee. He went into the crib to clean off. When he went back to the basement, Fatboy was smoking a joint and passed it to Teco. Teco said, "Fatboy, I need to walk around the corner. I'll be right back." Teco gave Fatboy some dap and went out the back door.

He walked up the street to reach Williams Avenue, until he found the right house. Teco walked up the steps and rang the doorbell three times before his sister, Kee, came to the door. She said, "Teco, stay right here on the porch. Okay?" Once she came back, she had a bag full of clothes and said, "You have to leave now because I'm the only person who can be in the house."

He gave Kee a hug and said, "Thanks sis."

When he got back to Fatboy's crib, he pulled the clothes out of the bag and was happy to see what Kee had given him. It contained a pair of Joe Palmarie jeans, a pair of shell toe Adidas, one pair of Top Ten Adidas, and two silk shirts to match the jeans. At the bottom, there was the Troop sweatsuit that he always wanted. Then Fatboy came in the basement and asked, "Damn Teco, where you get those fly rags from?"

"I just got them out of the trunk of the car. I'm gettin' ready to go on a skimmie mission." Teco got dressed and took off in the car headed down the street towards Vernon Road.

◊◊◊◊◊

Two weeks later, Teco was driving around at night, when he saw Blue standing outside the Chinese store. Blue flagged Teco down, as if he needed something. Blue walked up to the car and asked, "Whatz up, Teco?"

"Nothin' man, I'm just chillin'. Why whatz up?" asked Teco.

"I need you to do me a favor. Plus, I'll pay you." Blue just mentioning money caught Teco's full attention.

"Okay."

"I need you to take me to Germantown at 8 o'clock."

"I'll do that for you; but you know this ride is hot. Right?"

"Lil' homey, you don't have to tell me. I know how you do it."

Blue's real name was Carlos Johnson. The entire Johnson clan was over 6 feet tall, even the women. So Blue calling Teco little was pretty accurate, even though Teco was older than Blue. Blue's huge frame was all muscle. His large hands as well as feet stood out more than anything. Blue's super black skin tone made him look blue, which is how he got his nickname. At one time, Blue dated Teco's sister, Kee. Blue and Teco never saw eye to eye, because they were into different street games. They both gave each other respect. Blue was about selling dope; whereas, Teco was a car thief. He even tried to put Teco down;

however, Teco messed up some dope. Blue never dealt with Teco like that anymore.

Teco drove back to Fatboy's crib, until it was time to pick Blue up. Then he drove to Blue's crib, parked the car, and knocked on the door. Blue came to the screen door and said, "Teco hold on." So, Teco decided to wait for him in the car. In five minutes, Blue got into the Johnny.

"You ready?" asked Teco. They drove for ten minutes in silence. *"I wonder how much dope this homey got on him. Does he have a pistol? If we get stopped, we are through."*

Blue broke the silence. "Teco can you keep a bond wit me?"

"Yeah, why? Wassup?"

"There's this Narc that we call Shakey that keeps fuckin' wit me. He keeps stoppin' me every time he sees me and shakin' me down for money in order for me to sell dope ova in G-town." As they drove, Teco was looking out for any cops, because they would be passing by the precinct shortly.

"You mean the Narc wants you to pay him, so you can sell dope on the streets?"

Just as they were talking, Blue tapped Teco on the arm, pointed, and shouted, "There he is right there! Messing wit those dude's. Yeah, that's his fat ass."

"So, what do you want me to do?"

"Drop me off at the next corner." Teco did what Blue asked. Blue gave Teco $50; then Blue got out of the car.

"Yo, can you swing past here at midnight and pick me up?"

"Yeah, after I go to Ivy Hill Bar. Do you got any reefer?"

"Here are two bags."

Teco drove off headed back towards Mt. Airy so he could change clothes over Fatboy's crib. When Teco reached Fatboy's crib, Fatboy wasn't there. Therefore, Teco decided to go over to Tasha Moore's house. Tasha's long slender legs were her greatest attraction. She was a young woman who wore clothes which made her look a lot older than her age. Teco loved her dark Nigerian skin tone and the way her black hair rested gently on her shoulders.

After he knocked on the door, Tasha let him in just as he knew she would. Teco had a way of playing with women's minds. He wanted to see if he still had her like before and he did. Just as he finished changing into his new clothes, Tasha stepped to him about coming back to see her later that night. Teco didn't immediately answer. *"She is lookin' good wit that new hair-do."*

"So are you comin' back or what?" asked Tasha.

"I'll see after the bar. I'll make sure I call you first."

As he was looking in the bathroom mirror, she pulled up behind him and put both her hands on his waist. "Let me feel your sexy body, Teecoo."

"Girl stop trippin'," said Teco. He turned around. Then kissed her on the forehead and jetted.

On his way to the bar, he pulled over beside Temple University Stadium and rolled a fat joint to smoke. He needed a moment to collect his thoughts. What Blue told him about those Narcs was really jacked up. Blue needed to change street games and join his ranks. Teco felt a chill.

Then, he pulled back onto the road. At the bar, he noticed that there were only 25 people there. So, he left. He stopped at the A-Plus Mini-Mart, which was right next to the bar. He bought some gum and Newports. Then, he got back in the car to go pick up Blue.

As Teco drove down Stenton Road, he crossed Chew Avenue, which would take him right back behind Germantown High School. Two blocks from there was where he would pick up Blue. He pulled up to the corner and saw Blue bent over holding his stomach. "Yo man, get in. You a'ight?"

"Teco, you would never believe what happened to me."

"Let me guess. Somethin' to do wit that Narc?" Blue was still holding his stomach, bent over. Teco didn't see any blood, so he knew it wasn't that bad. However, Teco was a little nervous.

"Yeah, let me tell you what went down. I was at the crack house; and there was a knock on the door. I went to see who it was and it was that Narc. When I opened the door, the Narc put his gun in my face. Then he told me that I had ten minutes to meet him outside. Once I closed the front door, I went out the back and down the alleyway. As I was goin' up the block, he came out of no where in his car. So I ran long enough to swallow my dope."

"How much did you swallow?" Teco asked with great concern.

"Ten bags of powder. He caught me and put me in the back of his car. He took me to the precinct, as if he was lockin' me up. Finally, he told me what he wanted me to pay him. Then he let me go. Now my stomach is startin' to feel fucked up." Blue was bending over in the front seat.

"You want me to take you to the hospital?"

"No, just take me home. I'll be cool," said Blue still bent over.

Teco rushed him home and hoped Blue would get some help, because he didn't look well. At the house, Blue gave Teco $50, but barely said, "Yo, come see me tomorrow and we'll talk."

"A'ight, be sure you drank some milk," said Teco nervously.

It was 2am when Teco got back to the bar. When he walked through the door, he looked around. To his disappointment, there were now only 10 to 12 people at the bar talking. *Just like old heads. Full of shit,"* thought Teco.

Because he had the munchies, Teco left and went to the A-Plus Mini-Mart. The light-skinned man in the store wouldn't let Teco in, since it was after midnight. After hours, they started to serve customers from a thick bullet-proof plexiglass with a small swivel window that turned left or right. As Teco jarred on the door, the cashier waved him to the window. So, he walked to the window really cool.

"Yes, may I help you sir?" asked the cashier.

"Yes Sir, I know exactly what I want. Can you please gimme two minutes?"

"Young man, our policy is that we don't—"

Teco cut him off to avoid all the policy shit. "Sir please, all I need is two minutes to get what I need." He pleaded once more before the cashier let him in the store.

"Okay, you only have two minutes." As the guy turned the key, Teco waited for him to open the door and proceeded to the candy section. Just as he was putting stuff on the counter, the cashier asked, "What do you get out of going to that hell hole?"

"I go to have fun and dance wit women."

The guy ended up keeping Teco longer than expected and introduced himself as Reverend Adorson. Teco shared a lot with this guy, since he said that he was a minister. Teco even told him about not having a place to stay. As Teco was about to leave, Reverend Adorson said, "If you need my help in the future, you can find me right here." Teco gave him dap and then left headed to the pay phone on the corner.

As he dialed Tasha's number, it rang three times before she picked up. "Hello." She said sleepily.

"Wassup, you still looking for me to come by or what?"

"Yeah, are you comin'?"

"It all depends, if you cum wit me."

"Well, when you get here, we'll see. I'll leave the door unlocked, so hurry up."

When Teco got there, Tasha had on a large Eagles t-shirt; however, he could see that she had nothing on underneath. Once they reached her bedroom, Teco took off his clothes and got in the bed with her. He first rubbed her phatt ass and gave her foreplay. Before he started to make his move and out of the blue, Tasha yelled, "Teco wait. Wait! Before you put it in . . ."

"Wassup girl?"

"You need to put this Jimmy on. I don't know who you been bangin'." Tasha really burst Teco's mood. Teco never liked wearing Jimmies. He liked it raw and wet. All he wanted to do was just bust a nut and go to sleep. And that's exactly what he did.

The next morning Teco showered, got dressed, and hit the streets. He had Kee on his mind. So, Teco decided to check on his sister before he went anywhere.

As he drove up Vernon Road, he saw a lot of police and detectives walking around some crime tape. The crime scene trucks were parked in front of the Super Quick gas station. Inside the store, there was a body with a white sheet on the floor. Things in the store were scattered everywhere, as if there had been a struggle. After Teco parked the car, he walked up to the crowd.

"Yo, homey, what happened?" asked Teco.

"Some guy got killed in there last night."

"Do you know who or what happened?"

"Nope, not yet."

This cop came up to them, "Do any of you people know this guy nicknamed Blue?" Teco's heart dropped to his feet.

"Why might you ask?" Teco asked trembling.

"Because this Blue guy died of an overdose. He must have snorted too much powder last night."

As Teco walked, tears rolled down for his homeboy. He wiped his face, sucked it up, and pushed on knowing that it wasn't Blue's fault. There was no way that he would see Kee now, because he didn't want to be the one to tell her what happened to Blue. *"It was you muthafuckas that killed him."*

Just as Teco was about to cross the street, he heard a lady from CSI ask, "The street life, is it suicide or murder?"

CHAPTER 4

This was a very sunny day and things looked very promising for Teco as he drove up Baltimore Avenue. He didn't expect to pass by these two Narcs who knew him very well. They saw Teco before he saw them. By the time he passed them, it was too late; and they pulled right behind Teco's Johnny. *"Damn, I knew I shouldn't have come to this side of Philly."* Knowing that the car was on the hot list, Teco started to speed up reaching 45 to 50 mph in a 30 mph speed zone. With swift acceleration, Teco swerved to his left to avoid hitting the Southeastern Pennsylvania Transportation Agency (SEPTA) bus; however, Teco almost broadsided an oncoming car. At the corner of 58th and Baltimore Avenue, the police locked down the magnetized red light on top of the police car. Sirens were blaring throughout West Philly. As Teco crossed Fernwood Street, he brought down a stop sign trying his best not to crash into a car which was doubled parked.

When Teco got to 58th and Thomas Avenue, he pushed it to the floor bursting a right turn past the Children's Group Home. As he headed towards Cobbs Creek Parkway, another police car pulled in front of him attempting to cut Teco off. The only thing Teco could do was clip the bumper of the police car. Teco seized the opportunity to avoid capture by driving the car onto the sidewalk. When he hit the curb, his head slammed into the window. "Shit! Muthafucka!"

At Cobbs Creek Parkway, Teco hung a left giving him a straight away and another chance to loose the Narcs. When he thought he had the car under control, there was a red light coming up. Teco hoped that the light would change before he reached it; however, his timing was off. As he tried to slow down, the brakes locked on the car causing Teco to run onto the curb. He started to loose control. Teco found himself spinning around in the car, until it came to a complete stop. Coming in his direction were 5 police cars. Teco's car engine was still running; so he took off. Squealing tires could be heard blocks away. Teco jetted all the way until he got to 59th Street, where he could turn left going towards Chester Avenue.

At this point, Teco had them by two city blocks. On Chester Avenue, he made a left turn toward Kings Park. Once he reached the park, he drove the car in the parking lot and turned off the engine quickly. He wiped down the car really well. He ran to the bus stop across the street from the park, almost getting hit by a car, but reaching safety. While he stood at the bus stop, he had to decide what to do. Even though he didn't want to leave the Johnny, he couldn't stay at this bus stop long. *"Shit! What the fuck did I come out here for?"* The G Bus was coming his way; so he got on the bus and went back to 58th and Baltimore Avenue. Teco had to escape and find his homies. While on the bus, he noticed that his head was bleeding; however, this was nothing but a bump to Teco.

When he did reach the block, the streets were packed with all the neighborhood homeboys and homegirls. You could hear the rap music blaring from the big boom box on the stoop. Just as Teco stepped off the bus, he could see Stacy hugged up on some dude. From the corner of the block, everyone could see who was getting off of the bus. Before he could reach them, Cowboy said, "Yo Stacy, here comes Teco." Just at the sound of Teco's name, the dude with her froze up, as if he had seen a ghost. But it was too late, Teco had seen them together. She came walking up to Teco trying to explain herself.

Teco said, "I can't check you like you mine; but you betta gimme respect when I come 'round."

"Teco don't front on me out here," said Stacy.

"Look, let's go to your crib and chill. Do you feel like havin' some fun?"

"All you want to do is hit and run."

"Naw baby, it's not like that. I need to bounce. That's it."

After he smoked a joint and danced in the crowd with Stacy, they left the block together. They relaxed over at her crib until 6pm. As he got up, he realized that he never liked the fact that he had to catch the bus. Teco found it funny that he had the nerve to think that he actually owned the Johnny.

Teco didn't get off of the bus at the stop where the car was located. He went down to the next stop to get off. He wanted to see what the status of the car was. There it sat parked next to four other cars. As he walked, he saw that the car was unharmed; so he got in and drove off.

He went back to Mt. Airy headed towards Fatboy's crib. When he pulled up, Fatboy came to the car out of breath and asked, "Did you hear what happened to Blue?"

"Yeah, I heard. Plus, I was wit him the night he overdosed. I had just dropped him off at his house."

"That's fucked up he had to go out like that."

"Yep, you right. Hey look, I'll be right back. I need to find some weed." Teco drove off to Gerrets Lounge, across the street from Cheltenham Mall, to see if he could score some good bud. He pulled into the parking lot and jumped out. Just as he bent the corner, he ran into Aaron Woody. "Yo Aaron, wassup?"

"Yo Teco, what's rollin'?" asked Aaron. They greeted each other with some dap.

"Where can I get some good reefer?"

"I know where, but I have to take you there."

"Okay, let's ride." As they left the parking lot, Aaron told Teco to ride down Ogonz Avenue and make a left onto Upsal Lane. Just as he did a big blue patty wagon got behind Teco and turned on its top flashing lights. Teco wanted to mash out. He knew that the patty wagon couldn't keep up with him. As he thought to speed up, he realized that he was caught in the middle of rush hour traffic. So he had no choice but to pull over. *"Just my luck."* They could hear the cop on his bull horn say, "Please step out of the car real slow and put your hands on the hood."

Aaron stands tall with a gangster lean. His milk chocolate skin tone and his honey colored eyes were any woman's dream. With his big arms and large chest, Aaron carried his body weight well. His hair was cut neatly; and the closer you got to him, you could smell the CK1 cologne that he wore. Teco knew him from going to the Ivy Hill Bar.

This guy sold weed around the hood, Gerrets Lounge, and the mall. Teco could always find Aaron. The dope was Teco's only alliance with him. *"Aaron's on his own. Fuck that."*

They did as the cops asked. Immediately, the two cops came behind them and started frisking. When one of the cops bent over to shakedown Teco's ankle, Teco turned around quickly, smacking the cop's hand while spinning like a whirlwind.

Teco took off running. Brushing off the cop happened so fast that the cop looked perplexed as to what had gone down. Teco was lost in the wind. *"I got to duck these cops."* He ran all the way to the Ivy Hill Bar. When he got there, he knew he was safe. He pulled on the door but the bar was still closed. *"Shit! Shit!"*

He then went to the A-Plus Mini-Mart to get something to drink. As he opened the door, he saw the preacher dude behind the counter with a big smile on his face, as if he just hit the number. "Hello Teco."

"Yo, wassup Reverend?" Teco walked to get a pop out of the cooler.

"Is everything going alright today?"

Teco couldn't look him in the eyes, because he was too embarrassed to tell him what was really going on at that moment. There was one thing he would tell the Rev though. "Rev, I need a place to stay for a while."

Reverend Adorson looked at him for a long time and then said, "Look, this is what I'll do for you. I have a room at my place that I'll rent to you; but you must have a job." Teco looked at him in disbelief, not knowing what to say.

"I don't have a job right now, but gimme a few days and I'll have one."

"Or better yet, I may be able to get you a job working at this same company. Let me give you my address. Come by tomorrow; and you can move in with me. I need a little time to clean the room up." The Rev pushed a button on the cash register and a blank piece of white paper came out. He wrote down his address and gave it to Teco, who looked at the paper and left the store.

Teco really needed some time to pass, after running from the police. While he walked towards Fatboy's crib he started feeling like his life was futile. *"I can't keep livin' like this. I don't have a place to stay. I have gear this place and that place. It doesn't make any sense to be 21-years-old wit no place to call home."*

He reached Fatboy's crib with a despairing look upon his face. Mr. G. picked up on Teco's mood off the jump. "Teco let me see you for a moment." Teco had no idea what Mr. G. wanted, but he went anyway.

"Yeah Mr. G., wassup?"

"Why are you lookin' in that state?" Mr. G. asked in a concerned tone.

"Well to be truthful, I'm sick of livin' on the streets. And after what happened to Blue—"

"Look, the street cares 'bout no one. 'Always do what you always did; and you will always get what you always got.' I'll leave you that one to chew on."

He left Teco sitting right there on the steps. Teco heard Mr. G., but had other things on his mind. As he stood up, he knew that Mr. G. wouldn't let him stay tonight. So, he went to get his clothes from the basement and headed over to Tasha's crib. He had a few things over there as well.

When he walked up, Tasha was sitting on the steps with her German Shepherd. "Hey baby, wassup?" She asked.

"Do you mind if I stay here tonight?"

"You can stay; however, you have to leave before noon tomorrow." As she looked at him she knew something was bothering him.

"Teco, what's wrong wit you?"

"Nothin', I'm just ready to get my life together."

"Yeah, because you need to do somethin' other than steal cars and get high. Have you heard what happened to Blue?"

"Yeah, I heard and I refuse to go out like that."

After they talked for a while, he went in the house, took a shower, and went to bed. He didn't want to have sex or smoke any pot. The only thing he had on his mind was what Mr. G. said. *"Always do what you always did; and you will always get what you always got."*

CHAPTER 5

Two weeks later Teco was getting established. He even had a job working at the A-Plus Mini-Mart on 52nd Street across from Mr. Silks Bar. Reverend Adorson had put Teco down with this 3rd shift job to help Teco out. While at work it hit him that he did have a little peace of mind, even though the money was slow. Waiting for a pay check was something new; and Teco had to get adjusted. When he came in for work, he had to check the gas meters. He stuck a long 15 foot stick in the ground to see how much gas was in the tank. Then he counted the till for his shift. As Teco was working, he realized that he didn't smoke weed as often.

Teco was staying in the rough part of South Philly, with his new landlord, Reverend Adorson. The only rules the Rev imposed was that Teco couldn't have any women over and that he had to be in by 1am, unless he was working. *"I'm a grown man. Who the hell the Rev think he is talkin' to me like I'm in High School? Shit, I'm not havin' it. Those are two rules that I will break fo sho."*

One afternoon, Teco was chilling in his room, when the Rev knocked on the door. Teco was rolling some weed. "Yeah, just one minute." His landlord stood at the door trying his best to figure out what Teco was doing in there. Teco seldom came out and always had his door shut. Teco came to the door and asked, "Yes, how may I help you?"

"Teco, I've been meaning to speak with you about coming to my church this weekend."

"Sorry Rev, I don't do the church thing."

"Well, just think about it."

"Okay, I will do that." After the Rev walked away, Teco shut the door to his room and got dressed. He was planning to treat himself to the movies; but before he went to the underground subway, he smoked a fat joint.

While riding on the subway going to Center City, he thought about what his landlord said in regards to going to church. *"What could I loose?"* So, he made sure to remember and leave a note telling Reverend Adorson that he would go to church. The note stated, "Please wake me up for church."

On Sunday morning, the Rev smiled when he read the note. Unexpectedly, there was a knock on the Rev's door. "Come in."

"Hey Rev, man, I don't have any clothes for church. I know that people are gonna be up in there wit suits, ties, and Stacy Adam shoes. I don't have it like that."

"Don't worry about clothes. We'll deal with that later. Just put on something nice."

Teco decided to wear the Joe Palmarie jeans, the silk black shirt, and the black shell toe Adidas. He had to admit that he looked dapper.

When they arrived at the church, it seemed as if everybody knew that Teco was coming. They greeted him with open arms and love. Teco never felt like this before. He knew that he would be back to this church, which was fairly large. The main thing that intrigued Teco was the large number of young women.

This lanky man in a nice suit walked up to Teco and said, "Hello, my name is Pastor Williams." Pastor Williams reached out his hand for Teco to shake, but Teco's mind was elsewhere.

"I'm sorry what did you say yo name is?" asked Teco.

"Pastor Williams."

"Well, it's nice to meet you. I'm Teco."

"Teco, I would like to welcome you to our church."

"Thank you sir."

Teco went to have a seat so he could hear the message. The lady that sat next to Teco tapped him on the arm. "After church we have dinner in the basement." Teco felt that this was too good to be true. He had a place to live and food to eat. The same lady escorted Teco to the dinner; and the food was off the chain.

Teco had been going to church for three weeks. The Rev never had to ask Teco to be ready to go, because the congregation made him feel good. However, Teco still had personal issues, to include taking money from his job to support his bad habit of smoking weed. Plus, he still had the inner desire to steal cars.

On this particular Sunday, Teco decided to join the church. He was standing alone in the church vestibule in front of a mirror rubbing his hand over his wavy hair, when this female named Debbie Hines came up to him. "Hey Teco, how are you doin'?" He took a minute to give her a response, because he was checking out the curves and grooves in her dress. "Teco did you hear me?"

"My fault, I was somewhere else."

"Yeah, I bet you were," said Debbie. Once she noticed him looking at her, she put her hands on her round hips. While his eyes followed her hands all the way to her chest, she was adjusting her top. Teco realized that he was staring at her full dark lips. He had to pull himself out of the trance, before someone walked by them. Debbie talked about how she had been checking him out.

"What are you digging me for?" asked Teco.

"I was tellin' my mom 'bout you and how I was hopin' that we would join the church together." He could tell that she was a freak. She asked him to come meet her mom after church service. Teco agreed and said, "It has to be fast, because I don't want to miss my ride."

"I stay right ova there." She shifted him to a window and pointed to her crib.

"I'll only stay for a minute or two."

They went back into church and sat on two different pews. However, Teco's mind wasn't on the service nor was he trying to understand what was being preached. After the sermon titled "Yield not to Temptation," the pastor opened the doors of the church. Teco walked up to the front of the church with several other people. As he looked to see if any other people were coming, Debbie got up and stood beside Teco. *What is Debbie up to?*

The usher tapped him on the shoulder and asked, "Can you come out here and fill this out please?" He was given a membership card. While he was filling it out, he looked up; and there was Debbie coming in his direction to sit next to him to fill out her card. By the time they finished, church was almost over.

"This is a good time to leave." Debbie said. They both got up and walked out the side door. Just as she opened the house door, Debbie shouted, "Mom, Momma! Where are you?!"

"Girl, what are you calling me like that for?"

"I want you to meet Teco."

Her mother came into the living room with a big smile. "Hello son."

"Hello, ma'am, how are you?"

"Mom, this is Teco. Teco this is my mom, Mrs. Hines." He shook Mrs. Hines' hand, smiled, and then sat down. Debbie ran upstairs and returned with a baby boy. Teco looked at her as if he were asking, *"What the hell is this?"*

"Teco this is my son." The baby cooed with a smile. Then she took the baby upstairs.

When she came back down, Teco stood up. "I need to leave so I can catch my ride."

"Will I see you tonight at church?" asked Debbie.

"Yeah, I'll be there. See you then."

"Okay, peace out."

He kissed her on the cheek knowing that he had plans of sleeping with her very soon. As he reached the church, Teco's ride was just pulling up to take him to the Rev's crib.

Later that night, he went back to the church service as promised and back over to Debbie's crib. Teco couldn't stay long, because he had to go to work.

"Teco, will you come see me tomorrow, before you go to work?"

"Is that what you want from me?" asked Teco.

"Yes, I want to see you more."

"Well, I can do that," but deep inside he had no intentions of coming back to see her.

Teco left Debbie's house anticipating a very good night on the 3rd shift. While on the bus, Teco was only thinking about the fact that he had Debbie very eager to see him all of the time. After work, he went right home to get some rest. He was beat after getting off so early in the morning.

Teco slept all day. When he woke up, he headed to the bathroom, next to the Rev's bedroom. "Teco, I need to speak with you, when you get a second."

"What in the world do you have to talk to me 'bout now. You are already crampin' my style wit all these rules." After Teco washed his face and brushed his teeth, Teco knocked on the Rev's bedroom door.

"Come in Teco and have a seat."

Teco walked in, sat down, and looked very puzzled.

"I want to talk to you about that girl, Debbie. Are you dating her?"

Teco became very defensive. "Why are you askin' me that?"

"Because I saw you leave with her last night."

"I don't think that my personal life is any of yo business." Teco started to become very upset.

"Well look, if you arrive at church with me. You leave with me!"

Teco stood to his feet. "Man, you must be outta yo damn mind! I'm a grown man. You don't run me. Why do you care who I date any way? You need to get a life. As a matter of fact, I'm outta here!"

Teco walked to the door and slammed it behind him. He went to his room and got dressed. Once downstairs, he left the Rev's house to find Debbie. *"That mutha don't know who he's dealin' wit. He's lucky that I don't take his car."* Once at the subway, he sat in the back by himself. He hadn't planned on seeing Debbie today. However, Teco felt the need to talk with her about what just happened with the Rev.

He walked up to Debbie's door and banged three times. Debbie came to the door within a minute with her finger to her mouth and whispered, "Shusssh, my dad is upstairs. So be quiet."

He never noticed that all she had on was a blue button down men's shirt. Debbie's skin was the color of a Reese's Peanut Butter Cup. She had arched her eyebrows to perfection. Her bone straight hair gave her a cheerleader appearance. Teco could just imagine her doing a cartwheel and seeing that round ass in cheerleader bloomers.

They walked upstairs very softly. The baby was asleep; and Teco could barely hear the television show "Spencer for Hire" as they entered the room. "Have a seat," said Debbie. The only place to sit was on the bed. Teco knew right then and there that he would get some sex before he went to work. Teco always did remember what his father told him. *"Boy, if a woman sits on your bed for the first time, she's an easy fuck. If she allows you to sit on her bed for the first time, she's an easier fuck."* So, he knew what to expect tonight.

Once he sat down, then he really noticed that Debbie had nothing on underneath the blue shirt. She bent over and her pubic hairs on that fat pussy popped out. "Damn Debbie! Is it like that?"

She turned to Teco with a smile and asked, "Do you like what you see?"

"Hell yeah."

She came close to him and told him, "Open your legs." He did as she asked. She reached down between his legs and pulled out a plate from under the bed. The plate was heavily dusted with a white powder. He looked at her and asked, "What's that for?"

"For me and you if you want some."

"Hell no." He watched as she made a line using a white with red stripes plastic straw. With one sniff, the powder was up the straw and into her nose like a magic trick. After she did all of that, she came walking toward him very sexily licking her lips. "I want to give you some sex. This will make us feel a lot betta. It will numb yo body; and the sex will last longer. Trust me."

Teco had an inquisitive look on his face. "Okay, I'll try some." After he took two hits up his nose, he felt the chill all over his body.

He grabbed her on the ass; and as he did, his fingers melted at the touch of her skin. "Damn, your ass is soft."

She started pulling up his shirt and kissing him all over his neck. He couldn't believe that this was happening so fast. She grabbed his wood and let out a long passionate, "OOOh, I want to feel this inside me." She moved her hand down to his zipper and unzipped his pants. Once she had his zipper down, she looked him in the eyes, reached her hand in the secret compartment, pulled out his manhood, and caressed it with her soft long fingers. "Teco you have a nice size dick."

"You like how thick it is?"

"Yes, baby I do." Teco was sucking on her hard black nipples. As they walked backwards to the bed, there was a knock on the door. Knock! Knock! Knock! Teco got scared, froze up, and started to pull his pants up.

"Shusssh be quiet." Debbie went to the door.

Her mother said, "You need to quiet down in there."

He started taking off his clothes to get in the bed, but Debbie stopped him. "Let's lie on the floor." She put the cover down first and rested with her legs open. As Teco got on top of her, all he could see was that pretty pinkness. With the head of his wood, he could feel the wetness within her. He slid the head up and down making sure he hit that little man in the boat. "Baby stop playin' and put it in me." At her request, he slid all 7 inches deep into her until he couldn't go any further. She let out a long deep moan, "Oooh yes baby, it fits just right. Please take yo time." He started thrusting in and out slowly at first. Once Teco and Debbie found a combined rhythm, they began throwing themselves at each other.

"Ooh Debbie take this dick."

"Teecoo give it to me faster."

"No, No, I want you to remember that I was in you."

"Okay baby, let me turn ova so you can hit it from the back."

He pulled out of her wetness so she could get on all fours. He slid back in her with no problem. He could tell that she was starting to climax. She made long soft groaning sounds of pleasure, "Umm, umm, umm, baby jam that dick in my pussy." Teco pushed as she pushed. He was about to nut, but slowed down to slow stroke, which drove her crazy. She pulled away from him and changed positions. She got on top of Teco and started to ride him like a cowgirl. Her hands gripped his chest. She threw her head back, going faster and faster.

"Ooh shit! You go girl." He pushed up as she came thrusting down, pelvic to pelvic. With such driving passion, they both let out deep groans of pleasure.

"Dang, Teco you worked the shit out of me."

"I'm the one sweating." As she pulled off of him, he could feel nothing but that hot sticky wetness.

She got a damp warm wash towel from the bathroom and cleaned him off. As he lay there like a king, he started telling her about Reverend Adorson.

"You live wit him?" Debbie asked.

"Yeah, I rent a room in his crib."

Debbie paused and then said, "Uh oh."

"Debbie what?"

"I shouldn't gossip Teco."

Teco sat up. "Come on, you can't leave me hangin' like this."

"Teco, Reverend Adorson is gay."

CHAPTER 6

Teco stood up quickly off of the floor. "What the hell do you mean that he's gay?"

She named the gay men in the church. "Teco, you need to look out for them. You are handsome. They will start makin' passes at you."

Teco started to become very pissed off. The coke high, that he was on, started to come down. "Deb, I need to get ready for work."

She noticed his anger and started to help him button up his shirt. "Teco, let me talk to my mom and see if you can stay wit us for a while."

He knew that wouldn't work. She was trying to lock him down. He wasn't having that at all. Once he got dressed, he started to leave, but turned to give her a kiss. "I'll talk wit you later," said Teco.

While Teco was on the bus headed for work, all kinds of things ran through his head. He couldn't believe that he was living with a punk. As he thought more, he put two and two together. Things began to add up, such as why he couldn't have females over and why the Rev wanted Teco with him at all times. Teco even wondered if the Rev had a peep hole in the wall. The more he thought about this, the more upset and angry he became.

When he got to work, his co-worker said, "Hey Teco." Teco never heard her. He walked past her without saying one word. His mind was lost in thought. He went to the back office, sat in the chair, and stared at the wall. She found him and asked, "Teco did you hear me speakin' to you?" Teco was so into his own world that he didn't respond. So, she touched him on the shoulder. "Are you okay, Teco?"

He turned to look at her. "My fault, I have somethin' on my mind."

At first, she couldn't believe that he was ignoring her; after all, she was the best looking female employee at the A-Plus Mini-Mart. Then she said, "I wish I was that somethin' on yo mind."

Teco looked at her in shock. "You don't want to be."

He went to the safe to get a till in order to start the shift. The entire time he was making plans to get the Rev and break into the store safe. At this point, he didn't care about anything or anyone but himself.

The following night he was finalizing his plot, until he fell asleep for a couple of hours. When he woke up the next day in the early afternoon, he pulled the tray with the weed and the paper from under the bed. *"Well, it's time to make my move."*

After getting something to eat, Teco went into the living room where his landlord was sitting. "Rev, do you mind if I borrow yo car?"

He looked at Teco, reached in his pocket for the keys, and said, "Just be careful, please."

Teco really wanted to slide him in the face, but held his composure. When Teco got outside, he knew it would be at least 2 to 3 days before he would see the Rev's face again.

When Teco got into the car and started it up, the radio was tuned to WDAS, a local R&B station. Teco turned it to Power 99. He drove away at a high rate of speed and headed straight to his job to make a move on the safe. He pulled into the parking lot and noticed that there were only a few customers. Upon entering the store, Teco had a look of puzzlement on his face as if he had left something.

"Hey Teco," said the cashier smiling at him.

"Wassup? I left some keys in the back office. Have you seen them?"

She looked around the register and the counter with deep concern, as if she would find them. "Teco, I don't see any keys. They may be in the office."

His plan was flowing like water; therefore, he continued walking to the back office. More customers came into the store, which gave him ample time by himself. When he turned to where the safe was located, he smiled because the safe was cracked. Teco pulled out his trash bag from under his sweat jacket and filled it up with money. His adrenaline was rushing in full speed. As he left the office with the money, he held up his keys and said, "I found them by the VCR." Teco approached the car. *"Whew that was too easy."* Then Teco went straight to the spot on 52nd and Spruce Street, where he copped an ounce.

"I need to find a place to chill." As he was driving to find a hotel, he stopped at City Blues Fashion of New York for some gear. He went to the Gallery Mall to buy leather suits, a fur jacket, shoes, a Rolex timepiece, and two diamond rings. Teco was feeling real gangster by spending this free money. As soon as he left the Gallery, he drove directly to City Line Avenue. He checked into the best hotel in the area, which was the Comfort Inn. He decided to stay there for at least two weeks. Teco realized that his job would call the police; however, he really didn't care. *"Fuck those pooh butt ass pussies. See ya when I see ya."*

Teco still had the Rev's car. So, this was the perfect time for him to hit the streets and to enjoy himself by finding a skimmie to chill with him. Teco had a lot of money left, because he had hit the store up for 5 gees on this lick. Therefore, he decided to go out to Ivy Hill Bar, even though this was a huge risk of being seen by the Rev. He had a conscienceless way of thinking; however, he knew that he had to park the car a few blocks from the bar. From the back door, Teco entered the bar. The size of the crowd was nice. As he walked to the bar, he was checking out the ladies.

"May I have a pitcher of beer?" asked Teco.

"Will that be all?" asked the bartender.

Teco paid for the beer and sat down to scan the bar. He found one young lady sitting in the corner. This was the same skimmie, whom he had danced with before. He put a napkin over his pitcher. As he was walking to her table, he almost tripped over a piece of carpet. "Shit!"

Before Teco spoke, he took a sip of his beer. "Excuse me. I don't know if you remember me; but we danced once before. And we danced so well together that I was lookin' forward to seein' you again in here, hopin' that we could finish where we left off."

"I'm sorry, but I didn't know that we had started somethin'." She said.

"Well when we danced, we had danced five songs; and three of those songs were slow songs. When the music was ova, I left the dance floor with you havin' my full attention. You also have it now." She was looking at Teco and feeling him all the way. As Teco looked at her, he knew he had her. "Would you like to dance again?" asked Teco.

"Sure, but this time you have to buy me a drink after we dance."

Teco looked her in the eyes, as if he were penetrating her mind. He knew he was looking dapper with his new gear. Once Teco lifted her hand to help her out of her seat, he said, "Whateva it takes."

He led her to the dance floor. *"Damn she has nice soft hands."* Teco winked as she smiled back at him. She was average height with sexy bedroom eyes. Teco thought if he looked at her too long that she might put him in a trance. Her skin tone had a mahogany twist; and Teco loved dark-skinned women. *"I can't let her get away tonight."* He could tell that she was digging his flavor. He pulled closer to her in order to see how she would react. Just as he thought, she didn't back away. When he saw this, it was time to make his move. He gently placed his hands on her hips. "Are you ready for that drink? We have a long night ahead of us."

"Oh really?" she asked with a blushing look on her face.

They both looked at each other as if to ask, *"What next?"*

"My name is Teco."

"My name is Michele. My friends call me Me-Me."

"So shall I call you Michele or am I a friend to call you Me-Me?"

"Let me answer that later for you."

He smiled and grabbed her hand. "Let's order our drinks. Are you hungry?"

"A little."

"Well let's order some food also."

They enjoyed their food over great conversation. Teco was jonesing for a joint and needed to get away, but didn't want to be gone too long. "Excuse me but I need to step outside," said Teco.

"You leavin' already?"

"No, I'm steppin' out to smoke a joint."

"Do you mind sharin' wit me?"

"Well, to be honest I don't smoke wit strangers, only friends."

"Okay, I get the message. You can call me Me-Me."

"Let's go Me-Me." Teco gave her a real sexy smile as they both got up from the table. As they headed towards the door, he palmed Me-

Me's hand. He started walking towards the Rev's car, when she said, "My car is ova here."

They walked to her car and Teco said, "Oh, I see you like to be in the driver's seat. Get in your car, I'll be right back." He had the weed in the Rev's car. Teco came back to Me-Me within five minutes and could see her jamming to the music. As he approached, she unlocked the car door.

Me-Me started the car and Teco asked, "Yo, where are you going Me-Me?"

"I'm just pulling ova to the side of the bar."

"Okay, I thought you were tryin' to take me hostage." He reached in his pocket, pulled out a sack of reefer and rolled a fat one. "Here, fire this up."

"Did you have to make it so fat?" asked Me-Me.

"The fatter the betta, don't you think?" asked Teco in a deep sexy voice.

She looked at him out of the corner of her eye as she lit the joint. They smoked together and went back into the bar to continue the night. They danced some more and had a few extra drinks. Both were feeling relaxed. Marvin Gaye's song "Sexual Healing" came blaring out of the speakers.

Teco could tell that she was fucked up and ready to be pleased by him. As they danced, he held her so tight that Me-Me put her head on Teco's chest; and she moved his right hand from her waist to her butt. A bulge formed in his pants. Once he was fully erect, he softly brushed against the crest of her thighs.

"Oh, what's that in your pocket?" asked Me-Me.

Teco whispered in her ear. "I don't play pocket pool. It's all me, Me-Me."

She grabbed him tighter, letting him know that it was all good. Now that Teco had her attention, he asked, "Are you ready to leave?"

She lifted her head off of his chest, looked him in his eyes, and said, "Who said I was leavin' wit you?"

CHAPTER 7

"I was hopin' that we could end the night with some breakfast," replied Teco, who never gave her a chance to respond. He grabbed her hand, walked to the table to get her purse, and headed to the door. They walked at a steady pace and got into her car.

"Take me to my car," requested Teco.

"Why did you park two blocks away from the bar?" Me-Me asked.

Teco looked at her and said, "I'll tell you later, but what we can do is park yo car—"

"No Teco, just follow me; I live up the street."

Teco got into his car and followed her to Temple Avenue. When they arrived at Me-Me's house, she got out of the car. As she started up the steps, she yelled back to Teco, "I'll be right back!" She came out with a little bag and walked up to the Rev's car.

"Let me ask you what's in the bag," said Teco.

"If you must know, some little girl stuff. I thought that, if I've gone this far, we can end this night real nice."

"Okay that sounds perfect for me. But, before we go to eat, I need to drive to South Philly and pick up some clothes. Hop in."

He drove up Broad Street until he reached Catherine Street. As he passed ten row homes, he found a parking spot and pushed the button to release the trunk.

"Just gimme a few minutes." Teco went into the Rev's crib and turned on the lights. Me-Me could see his silhouette moving about in the crib. Within ten minutes, he came back with a small cigar box in one hand and gave it to her. "Roll us a joint."

As he started to put things into the trunk of the car, the police slowly rolled down the street. Teco played it off calmly, as if there were nothing wrong.

"Who do you live with here?" asked Me-Me.

"Well, I was rentin' a room here; but due to my job's location, I stay in a hotel on City Line Avenue.

"Teco, what do you do?"

"I'm a Rental Car Consultant."

"So, where are we gonna eat?"

"Since you have your little girl's bag, we can eat at the hotel diner."

Teco was hoping that she would not ask any more questions. They pulled into the driveway of the Comfort Inn Hotel. He parked the car and got his things out of the trunk while Me-Me carried the cigar box. Once in the hotel, he pushed the elevator button and went to room 307. They put everything in the room and headed right back down for breakfast.

Teco ordered a breakfast for two. When they finished, Teco escorted her back to the room. Me-Me asked, "Do you mind if I take a shower?"

"No, help yo'self," replied Teco.

"Would you like to join me?"

"No, you go ahead without me. I need to hang my things up."

"A'right, you'll miss me playin' in the water."

Teco ignored her and began to put his things away. As he sat on the bed, he picked up the phone and dialed zero.

"Hello, is this the Front Desk?" asked Teco.

"Yes, how may I help you, Mr. Jackson?"

"Do I have any messages?"

"You have two. Tina said call her at home. Fatboy said give him a call also. Will that be all, sir?"

"Yes, thank you." He hung up the phone and picked it back up to call Tina; however, he changed his mind and sat the phone back down on the hook. He knew Tina would want to talk on the phone and Me-Me was in the bathroom.

Me-Me came out in a red thong parading over Teco. She stood in front of the T.V. as if she were the Queen of Sex. "Is this what you wanted to see?" asked Me-Me.

He looked at her sexy chocolate body, which sparkled from the light. She had put baby-oil all over herself making her even more desirable to Teco.

"I really want to see if you can hang," remarked Teco.

"It's only one way to find out."

"Gimme a minute to take a shower."

"I'll be right here. Can I roll me a joint?"

"Sure, help yo'self."

"Do you mind if I toot some powder?"

"No, I don't. Do yo thing." As he was going to the shower, he thought, *"Do all fine ass women snort coke these days?"* While the hot water beat upon his body, he wondered how he was going to handle things as the money got low. In addition, he was in very deep thought about what to do with the car. Teco was drawn back into the moment by Me-Me's voice calling his name.

"Teco, Teco, Teco! Do you hear me callin' you?"

He emerged from the bathroom with just a towel wrapped around his waist and asked, "Yo, wassup baby?"

"I was wonderin' what was takin' you so long." He climbed on the bed crawling right between her legs. He kissed her with deep passion.

"Pass me that joint," said Teco.

"Do you want some of this blow?"

"Yeah, I'll take a little." After they smoked and snorted, Me-Me thought the coke would cause Teco not to get hard; however, it never hindered his performance. Just as Teco had planned, he started to break her off proper. He knew that she couldn't take too much of his dick. He had her running away from him in a playful way. As he packed his wood in her, she asked, "What are you tryin' to do to me? This is some good dick, Teecoo."

Without a word, he smacked Me-Me on the ass. She loved it. As he pushed, she pushed. Teco wanted to finish, so he could get some sleep. However, he never half stepped when it came to sex and enjoyed seeing women get off first. He would never allow a woman to fake an orgasm, because he took them to the limit, climax after climax. Just as she thrust harder, he slowed her down and turned her on her back.

As he maneuvered back into her, he made the head of his wood hit the top of her pussy by aligning his pelvis over her pelvis. As he did, she let out a loud scream, "Teco! Teco, yes, baby, hit it. You're right on that spot. Oooh, oooh, I'm comin' Teco!" Her body started shaking as he pumped that G-spot. They both came at the same time. Knowing that Me-Me was totally satisfied, Teco fell asleep on her chest.

On the following morning as he woke up, there was a wet warm caressing sensation making his wood come to a full stiff erection. Once he was fully awake, he looked down and there was Me-Me. Her head was bobbing up and down putting all 7 inches in her mouth. When he was about to bust a nut, she moved up and sat on his wood riding him as if she were going somewhere. Allowing him to explode, Me-Me said, "Oh Teecoo, I love this dick. You can fuck this pussy anytime."

Teco took a few minutes to hold and talk to Me-Me. Then he said, "Me-Me, let me get you back home." On the way to Me-Me's crib, she gave Teco a goodbye kiss and told him every way that he could reach her. *This can't be the same woman, who just said a few hours ago, 'Who said I was leavin' wit you?'*

Back at the hotel, Teco was getting out of the shower and heard the phone ring. *Who the hell is this?*

"Hello."

"Teco, how are you doin'? This is Tina."

"Wassup Tina? I was just thinkin' 'bout you."

"Is that right? Well, you are a hard man to reach. Well, I was in the area and wondered if I could stop by?"

"Now's not a good time. I've just got out of the shower—"

"That could be a good sight." Tina and Teco laughed.

"Anyway, as soon as I get dressed, I'm on my way out the door."

"When you get back, gimme a call."

"Maybe we can hook up later."

Teco placed on the bed a black leather suit and a pair of Stacy Adam ankle boots. He put on the Rolex and both rings; the only thing missing was a model on his arm. Once he was dressed, Teco looked in the mirror and smiled. *"Damn I look good."* His smile dropped when he thought about the uncertainty of his next move, given the fact that he had no place to go.

◊◊◊◊◊

He had been in the hotel for three weeks now; and his cash flow was really low. On his way out of the hotel, there was a Front Desk Clerk that caught his attention. She smiled as soon as he glanced her way.

"You look good today." She said.

"Thank you. And you look lovely every day."

"Can I see you when you get back later?" she asked.

"Sure just gimme a call in my room." Teco enjoyed flirting with the skimmies, always trying to find him a new dimepiece.

The day was nice and sunny with kids playing outside and having huge fun. He drove to Fatboy's crib to see what he was doing today. Mr. G. opened the door.

"Hello, Mr. G. Is Fatboy in?"

"You know where he is with his lazy ass."

Teco went downstairs to the basement. There was his homey lying on the bed like he had a hang-over. Teco shouted, "Yo! Yo! Get yo lazy ass up."

Fatboy never moved one inch, so Teco looked for something to play with in Fatboy's ear. Teco picked up a piece of string and stuck it into Fatboy's ear. Fatboy smacked his ear really hard. Smack! Teco did it again. Smack! Smack!

"Get up Fatboy!"

"Yo man, why you playin'?"

"Look I'm gettin' ready to go 'round the corner and see my sista. Be up when I get back."

"For what homey?"

"Man it's nice as hell today. We need to hit Cheltenham Mall. Then we will hit the Gallery. So be up when I get back."

"Yeah, okay. Man, just chill."

Teco went out of the back door and over to Williams Avenue, where his sister Kee was staying. He didn't see any cars in front of the house. He rapped on the door three times anyway. He heard a man say, "Hello. Who is it?"

"It's Teco, Kee's brutha." Teco could hear the keys turning on the other side as the door opened. The same guy that was at the bar a few days earlier opened the door and looked Teco up and down.

"Do you have a heater?" asked Bashi.

"Hell no."

"Well, come in and have a seat." Once Teco stepped inside the house, his eyes lit up because everything was so lavish. He never saw paisley velvet cloth wallpaper. There was a big screen T.V. and a playpen sofa. As Teco sat down, he crossed his legs as if he were the big Don Juan.

"My name is Mujaheed Bashi Fiten. Everyone calls me Bashi. I don't think we've met yet, but I have heard a lot 'bout you."

"I must say that my sista does know my ways."

Bashi reminded Teco of a younger version of Billy Dee without the hair. For someone 26 years old, Bashi lived a plusher lifestyle than people who worked for 30 years and retired. To women, Bashi's body looked like an artist had chiseled his physique. Outside of his SB life, Bashi enjoyed laying bricks in the summer and cutting wood in the winter. He was stronger than any member of SB or YBM; and nobody fucked with him or his family. Bashi handpicked who was a member of his SB Crew. He didn't mind taking exceptional talent off of the streets and providing a home for them. His soft heart was his only weakness.

"Yo sista Kee will be back later. Look, let me ask you a question. Will you take me to the bank in Willow Grove?" asked Bashi.

"Sure, when do you want to go?"

"Can you take me in 20 minutes?"

"Yeah, I'll be back in 20 minutes."

Teco went back to Fatboy's crib. When he got there, Fatboy wasn't dressed yet. "Yo, Fatboy, I need to take Bashi to the bank. You need to be dressed when I get back or you'll be left."

Teco drove the car around the corner, parked in front of Bashi's crib, and hit the horn. Bashi came out with a small leather bag. Teco said, "Yo, before we ride, you should know that this ride is a Johnny."

"You just handle yo business Teco."

45

Teco drove off headed towards Willow Grove. Bashi told him where to go; and they arrived at the bank with no problem.

On the way back Bashi said, "Teco, I want you to think 'bout somethin'. You don't have to ride like this. If you want to make some good cash flow, let me know. I'll put you on my crew."

"I respect the offer, but I don't sell dope."

"Who said you have to sell dope? When you are ready, let me know." When Teco dropped Bashi off, Bashi gave Teco $200.

"I can do this more often."

CHAPTER 8

As he turned the corner Fatboy was sitting on the steps smoking a Newport. "Yo, come on. Let's ride," said Teco.

They were at the mall trying to get as many digits as they could. Teco and Fatboy had been there 2 hours. Before they went downtown to the Gallery, they pulled over at Huntington Park to smoke some weed. While they were smoking, a Narc pulled up and said, "Yo, that don't look or smell like a Newport."

Fatboy snatched the joint out of his mouth and said in a rushed tone, "Yo Teco, it's time to roll." Teco and Fatboy got back into the car, hit Broad Street, parked at Spring Garden Street, and walked the rest of the way to the Gallery.

As they ate at McDonalds, Teco and Fatboy made cat calls at women. Fatboy captured the attention of a cute young lady with much definition. She willingly gave Fatboy her number and allowed him to give her a kiss on the cheek. Fatboy had a smooth way of enticing women into surrendering that kiss, which was a technique Teco tried only once. Teco remembered getting smacked; so he never tried Fatboy's move ever again.

Teco was thinking about Tina. "Yo, I need to make a call. I'll be right back." Once he found the pay phones, he dialed her number.

"Hello, may I speak with Tina?"

"Hold on one moment."

Tina answered the phone sounding like she was asleep and said, "Hello."

"Wassup baby?"

"Who is this?"

"It's Teco."

"Hey, wassup baby? I didn't think you would call back."

"Look, once I get to the hotel, I'll call you. And maybe you can come see me."

"Well, I need to start gettin' ready. How long will it be before you get to the hotel?"

"Gimme 2 to 3 hours."

Fatboy and Teco walked around the Gallery one more time; then they left. Teco noticed that Fatboy had 7 telephone numbers and that he had only 3. As they stopped at the Water Ice stand, Fatboy asked, "Hey Teco. Who did you call?"

"This skimmie I met at the car wash. Her name is Tina."

"Wassup wit Tina?"

"I'll find out later tonight." Teco was really looking forward to seeing her.

After dropping his homey off, Teco headed back to the hotel and stopped at Pathmart to pick up some beer, ice cream, and some chips. Then he went to the pay phone to call Tina to let her know the deal.

As soon as he shut the door to his hotel room, the phone rang.

"Hello."

"This is your new friend," said the woman.

"Oh Really?" asked Teco.

"Yes Really."

"Does my new friend have a name?"

"Yes, Rhonda Hopkins. Can I come see you?"

"Sure but I'm expectin' company within the next hour."

"That's fine. I won't keep you long."

Five minutes later, there was a knock on the door. There stood Rhonda, who walked in as if she were owed the right to be in his presence. For the most part, that turned Teco on. He liked a challenge; and for some reason, he saw her as one.

Rhonda was not one of Teco's normal picks, because she had a sweet personality. Rhonda wasn't a chump off either. She was thick with a firm ass. He liked the way her auburn brown hair bang swept across her face and behind her ear. She was a touch of class from Boston.

"How are you doin' Mr. Clean?"

"I see you have jokes."

"So Teco, how long are you gonna be at the hotel?"

"Why do you ask?"

"Just wonderin' how long I have to make my move." She replied.

"If you ask me, you have already."

"No, when I make my move you will know it 'cause it will be direct."

"Well excuse me. You don't mind if I get undressed in front of you? I need to take a shower. I am as you say, Mr. Clean."

"No, you go right ahead."

Teco started taking off his shirt. He noticed that she became real fidgety, when he got down to his blue bikini briefs.

"I think it's time for me to go. Remember, I'm still workin'."

"Okay, let that be the reason."

As she stood up, he moved closer to Rhonda. Her eyes were affixed on the bulge in his briefs.

"Do you like what you see?" asked Teco.

"I'm sorry, but excuse me?" Rhonda asked without moving. Teco got so close that the bulge was now on her. Rhonda continued to say, "I think you should back up before—"

"Before what?" asked Teco.

Rhonda maneuvered her way towards the door. Just as she touched the door knob, Teco spun her around, pinned her against the door, pressed his body on hers, and gave her a soft kiss. Rhonda thought, *"Damn he's good."*

Once he stopped kissing her, Teco said, "Take that with you until I see you later."

Rhonda licked her lips and replied, "Sure will." She composed herself and left the room.

Then Teco took the shower. *"What is Rhonda's motive or is she a real freak?"* As he dried off, he was thinking about Tina, as well as what Bashi offered him. Then there was a knock at the door.

He put the towel around his waist, opened the door, and asked, "Hey, wassup girl?"

Tina walked in with a big smile, put her little bag on the table, and sat on the love seat. "I was dropped off by my brutha. So you will have to take me back in the mornin'," said Tina.

"That's cool wit me. By the way where do you stay?"

"Do you know where Bartrum Village is?" He would have never guessed that she lived in the Village, which is the true hood of hoods, real gutter.

"Yes, I know 'bout the Village. Do you mind if I only have on a towel?"

"I prefer you put somethin' on."

He was trying her in order to see if she were easy bait. At her request, he put on a blue velour robe. He had two beers as they watched television. Believe it or not he fell asleep, lying on her chest. She was very fond of Teco for not trying to sex her up. If she only knew that he was just tired as hell. Other than that, he would have been all over her trying to bang her back out.

The next morning came quickly. It only seemed as if he had 3 hours of sleep. When he woke up, Tina was watching television.

"Tina, what time is it?"

She reached for his Rolex watch. "It's 10 o'clock." He put both of his hands over his face, stretched, and reached for a joint.

"Do you smoke weed, Tina?"

"No, I believe in being drug free."

"That's cool too. That's more for me." He rolled a joint. While he smoked it, he blew smoke in her face trying to give her a little contact. She smacked him on the arm. In turn, he laughed at her, grabbed her, and slammed her playfully on the bed. "Teco stop, you play to ruff."

He walked to the bathroom to wash his face and brushed his grill. When he turned around, Tina was standing right in front of him. She pushed herself against him, threw her tongue in his mouth, and palmed his butt to pull him closer.

"You feelin' quite frisky this mornin'," said Teco.

"Is it anything wrong wit that? I think you deserve a treat."

"Is that right? And what did I do to deserve this treat?"

"All the right things."

Teco wanted to have sex with her, just to smack that phatt ass. However, he also wanted her to know that her pussy didn't move him. Teco enjoyed the mind control, knowing that any other guy would have jumped at the chance to fuck her.

"Tina, would you be upset if I had my treat at a later date?"

No man ever turned down a chance to sleep with her. This really made her want him even more. "I was just testin' you to see if you would jump at the chance, makin' this a sex thing. You passed that test." But deep inside and outside, she was wet in her panties wanting him to slide his wood in her. She knew that he would be a good fuck. So instead, they both got dressed; and Teco took her home.

Teco didn't like the Village very much, because it was one way in and one way out. That made him an easy target for the Robbing Crew. Once he dropped her off, he left trying to get out of the Village rather quickly.

He headed towards Mt. Airy. While at the light, the car shut off. He turned the ignition to start it again; however, the car moved slowly. Teco had the pedal all the way to the floor, but other cars were passing him. Even though he knew what was wrong with the car, Teco decided to abandon it anyway. He got all of his things out and walked up the street. He walked to the 8300 block of Williams Avenue. *"Now whatcha gonna do?"* He needed to reach the hotel.

He remembered that Me-Me lived nearby on Temple Avenue. So, he walked to her crib and knocked on the door. This young guy came to the door and said, "Me-Me isn't in."

"Isn't this a bitch." Teco left Me-Me's house, went to the bus stop, and waited for the bus. Teco hated Public Transportation the most.

Back at the hotel later in the evening, Rhonda was at the desk and winked at Teco. Teco returned her secret hello with his hand up to his face in the shape of a phone and motioned *"Call me."* She nodded her head to reply okay.

Once in the room, he started getting his things together, because he knew that he wouldn't be able to stay at the hotel much longer. When the time was right, he needed the ability to quickly pick up in order to go.

Then, the phone rang and Rhonda was on the line. "You have some messages. Would you like for me to tell you what they say?"

"Sure, go ahead."

"Tina said she had a nice time last night; please call. This is from Me-Me, who says that she is sorry that she wasn't in and to please give her a call. Last but not least my message, this is Rhonda; I will be up there in ten minutes." Click, she hung up.

"Hello. Hello . . ." He started moving the stuff off of the bed as fast as he could. He didn't want her to know that he was packing.

The room was looking pretty normal when there was a knock on the door. Simultaneously, the phone rang. "Hold on, I'll be right there." Teco said to Rhonda while picking up the phone.

"Hello," said Teco.

"Yo, wassup Teco? I need to tell you somethin'," said Fatboy.

"Before you say anything hold on, I need to open the door."

Teco said to Rhonda, "Come in and have a seat." Then he picked the phone back up and asked, "Fatboy, you still there?"

"Yeah, what skimmie you got there now?"

"The one from the front desk. Wassup?"

"I was at the Ivy Hill Bar last night and two detectives came in askin' questions 'bout you. I told them that you are from N.Y."

"What the hell you do that for?"

"To have them believe that you may have went back to N.Y."

"Okay, that's cool . . . . Yo, I lost the car. I'll tell you 'bout it . . . . Look, let me get up with you later." Teco decided that he would tell Rhonda that he couldn't talk. *"It's time to relocate."*

"Sorry Rhonda, I had to handle that first. Listen—"

"Well, I only have one hour for lunch; and I was hopin' I could have you," said Rhonda with an inviting look on her face.

Teco looked at her with a smile. "Well sure you can. Where would you like to start eatin'?"

CHAPTER 9

Teco had been M.I.A. for six weeks. He was living with Rhonda in Overbrook by Dobbins High School. The only thing Teco did wrong in Rhonda's eyes was smoke weed. She thought of him as an honest person, but little did she know about Teco.

As her first live-in boyfriend, Teco had her head really fucked up. He did things to her that no man had ever done before. She was 24-years-old and didn't have her first piece of wood until she was 21. She had never been a climatic person until she met Teco. He had a way of making women climax more than once while engaging in their sexual body exercise; and Rhonda was no exception.

Teco needed to talk with Bashi, but had no way over to his crib. *"I wonder if Rhonda will let me use her car."* He got enough balls to walk into the kitchen and ask her.

"Hey baby, can I use yo car?" Teco asked with calmness. At first, she looked at him as if he were crazy; but then her look softened.

"Sure baby the keys are ova there."

He went to get dressed; and as he was leaving, he gave her a passionate kiss. "I'll see you when I get back."

He drove right to Bashi's crib. He rapped four times before GQ, Bashi's right hand, came to the door. Gail Indigo Que, a.k.a. GQ, was a modeling agency's dream. If her friends didn't know any better, they would have thought she was from Somalia, Africa. Men longed to touch her silky brown hair and to caress her sienna smooth skin. Her long supple legs would have been the envy of dancers, if she could have afforded to take the classes. Her eyes were an ophthalmological mystery. Depending on the lighting, her eyes appeared hazel, or light-blue, or almond-blue in the light.

Teco saw GQ as a true tom boy. He never experienced her feminine side. She only wore hooded sweat shirts with boy cut jeans. She was tough and didn't take shit off of anyone. Her kick ass attitude along with her cornrow hair made her look like a true butch. She was qualified for the position in SB. That's why Bashi trusted her in everything and why she was the one who managed the runners.

At the door, GQ gave Teco an evil look and said, "Yo, wassup? Ya sista ain't here. She moved out and said somethin' 'bout D.C."

"You think I don't know my own fam moved to D.C.? I came to see Bashi."

"For what?"

"That's between Bashi and me." At that moment, GQ didn't like Teco, because she always wanted straight answers.

"Hold on," said GQ, who shut the door leaving Teco outside.

Bashi opened the door and said, "Come in. Wassup Teco?"

"Nothin', can I speak to you alone?"

While Teco was talking with Bashi, Teco was looking GQ eye to eye. Teco didn't like her either and it showed. Bashi saw the friction and smiled.

"Come up to my room," said Bashi. Teco and Bashi both went upstairs as Bashi led the way.

Once Teco was in the room sitting in the chair, he said, "Look Bashi, let's be up front. I need some work."

Bashi leaned back to examine Teco's sincerity in wanting to make some cheese. "Are you for real 'bout this?"

"Hell yeah."

"Okay, you must first show up here tomorrow at twelve noon. Then we'll sit down and talk more."

"Thanks Bashi."

"Don't thank me now. Let's see if you are up to makin' your money as you say. Oh, don't come here with a Johnny." Looking Bashi in the eyes before leaving, Teco gave him a firm handshake.

On the way to Rhonda's crib, Teco had a big smile on his face and was in a tremendously good mood. He knew nothing about this side of the street life. However, he was about to learn the hard way and learn it very fast. Either you become what they are or you die from being in the way.

On the next day, Teco really wondered what Bashi had to talk about. He had Rhonda drop him off over to Fatboy's crib. Then Teco walked around to Bashi's crib. Bashi was in the backyard with his rottweiler when Teco walked up.

"Yo, wassup?" asked Teco.

"Yo, come 'round to the front gate," said Bashi.

"Hold that dog, man." Teco wasn't afraid of dogs; but this dog was huge.

"He won't bother you. Here, come pet him." Teco walked over to the dog; and just as he got closer, the dog jumped on Teco almost knocking Teco down.

"Yo, be careful; he's real strong," warned Bashi.

"Now you tell me," said Teco sarcastically.

Bashi laughed. "Yo, come on in the house."

They went through the back door into the basement, which was GQ's luxurious room. Once upstairs, Bashi told Teco to have a seat in the living room. He explained to Teco the deal and talked with him for hours.

Bashi is down with YBM. His crew is known as SB, which is a four member crew. Bashi would never hustle dope in Philly because that territory belongs to YBM and the Italians from South Philly.

"Look, I have no time for any bullshit or games. If I bring you in, you roll with my rules. I send the crew out every morning with a $2000 bomb. You get 25 off each 100."

"I thought you said I won't have to push any dope?"

"I want to try you out on the block, before I bring you in. Are you game for that?"

"I'm in."

"This dope spot is jumpin' and there's no way you shouldn't get your bomb off. Whateva you don't sell is yours and is deducted from yo profit at the end of the night."

"Where's this spot?"

"Have you ever heard of Conshohocken, Pennsylvania? It's Right outside of Philly close to Norristown."

"No, I've never heard of Consho-who?"

Bashi laughed and said, "Don't worry. I'll show you later." He filled Teco in on the rest of the do's and don'ts of SB. He showed Teco that they wear an onyx diamond ring with SB raised in the middle.

"Once you're in, then you'll get one and more."

Teco couldn't wait, because he was about to get paid and shine like the big boys.

"Yo, let's ride. I need to meet wit someone. Have you ever carried a heater?"

"Yeah, that's no problem." Teco knew he was lying. He never had reason to play the gun role. He gave Teco a loaded black snub-noise .38.

"Watch my back. If anyone makes a move as if I'm in danger, you know what to do."

Teco knew right then and there that he was out of his line of crime. *"What the hell have I gotten myself into?"*

Bashi watched Teco pack the heater. Teco had no idea that Bashi was just testing his heart. The next step was for Teco to go to YBM, so that the boys could see Teco for approval.

They drove to the 8500 block of Temple Avenue. Teco got out of the car first looking for anyone standing around appearing out of place. Bashi was observing how alert Teco was at that moment. Teco stood on the driver's side with his hand on the heater; and his heart was racing 100 miles a minute. Sweat rolled off of Teco's head in little beads, as he walked Bashi to the front door of YBM's crib.

When the front door swung open, a guy stood there with a pistol. Teco pulled his .38 out ready to aim and fire; however, Bashi raised his arm across Teco's chest stopping Teco from raising the .38.

"Teco, it's cool. Put it up." Teco hesitated for a moment and then put it up. "Go wait in the car, Teco. I'll be a few minutes." While Bashi was inside, Teco never got into the car.

"So what do you think?" Bashi asked the YBM Crew.

"I see he don't ask any questions," said Yusef, who was the enforcer for the YBM Crew.

"Yeah, I like that 'bout him too," said Bashi.

"Give the little homey a chance; but if he fucks you, rock his ass," said Lil' Tim, the boss of the YBM Crew.

"Yeah, I know the rules," said Bashi, who would make sure that he personally taught Teco all the ropes.

"By the way what's his name?" asked Yusef.

Bashi replied, "Teco, but I'm gonna call him Homicide. He reminds me of a younger version of you, back in the day."

"Is he a killer?" asked Basil.

"I don't know yet, but I'll find out." Bashi gave them some dap.

As Teco and Bashi drove back to the crib, Teco asked, "Bashi, let me ask you somethin'. Who were those guys?"

"That was the head men from YBM." Teco became nervous not knowing what to expect next. Bashi continued to say, "Teco you got some real heart not knowin' who they were. I know you would have my back if need be."

"Yo, I'm real 'bout what I do."

"Look now, I need to tell you this. Everybody likes you; but the only condition is that you have to move in wit the crew. You're not a part of YBM and don't let that come out yo mouth. You down wit SB. Do you have a problem wit that?"

"No, but I have one question."

"What's that?"

"Do I have to let you know my every move?"

"Well, that all depends."

"On what?"

"If it deals wit makin' money off of my products, yes. If it deals wit yo personal life, no. But know who you dealin' wit."

As Teco chilled at the crib with Bashi for a few more hours, Teco decided to call Rhonda.

"Yes, may I speak with Rhonda Hopkins?"

"Speakin'."

"Wassup baby?"

"How are you Teco?" She paused and said, "I'm missin' you."

"Is that right? Well, do you think I can get you to play wit that kitty kat?"

"Why play with her when she's wet already?"

"How long before you get off of work?"

"In forty-five minutes."

"Can you come and pick me up? Let's see what we can do 'bout that wetness of yours." She laughed and then hung up the phone.

Teco called out to Bashi, who was upstairs. "Hey Bashi, I'm leavin' to go ova to see my homeboy, Fatboy!"

"Teco, come see me in three days. Be ready."

CHAPTER 10

Teco had to tell Rhonda that he was moving out; however, he knew that she wouldn't understand. It was the day that he was supposed to move into the SB Crew crib. He hadn't packed his clothes yet, not as if he had a lot to pack.

While Rhonda and Teco sat at the table eating breakfast, Teco said, "Rhonda, I need to talk wit you."

"What is it? You have been actin' real funny."

"Now, I don't want you to be upset wit me but, but . . ." Teco said stumbling all over his words. He got really quiet, because he knew she would trip. *"Is she in love wit me or is she in love wit the sex?"*

"But what Teco?"

"I need to move out and take care of some business."

"Oh, you got another bitch? You tryin' to move in wit her?" Rhonda stood up from the table, as if she were about to flare on him right there. He raised his head up to be on guard for any punches.

"I took care of you all this time and this is the thanks I get?"

"Now, sit your ass down and chill out, so you can hear me out first."

Rhonda left the kitchen and stormed into the living room.

"Rhonda, don't walk away from me!" Teco got up and ran behind her to explain his move. He knew he had to be honest with her for all that she had done for him. Teco grabbed her by the arm and said, "Stop and please listen to me. If you love me as you say, hear me out."

Rhonda looked out the window, never making eye contact with him. "I'm listenin'. Make it good."

He said, "See baby, in order for me to be a part of this crew, I have to live wit them. Wit this break, things will be promisin' for us in the future. I'm not leavin' you."

"Teco, I hear what you are sayin', but that life brings nothin' but death. I don't need the money."

He knew she was serious, because she never cracked a smile.

"Rhonda, I'll keep you up to date on everything. I'm not takin' my clothes. I want you to hold my money for me. This crew will never know about you or where you live just in case I need to get out. Now, gimme a kiss."

"Can I have some of that good dick before you go? I know it will be a while before I see you again."

"You act like I'm goin' to Japan. Well, if that's how you feel, then let me give you some Ching Chong stick." Then, Teco smacked her on the ass, as they went upstairs.

Later that day, Rhonda drove Teco to the SB crib.

Teco said, "This is where I'll be stayin'. Remember this crib. Rhonda, tell NO one."

"Baby, you know I won't tell anyone."

Teco asked Rhonda to pull over to the curb. Rhonda said, "Teco, call me every night."

As Teco made sure that she drove away, he headed to Bashi's crib. One black SS Monte Carlo, two Mercedes, and one red Porsche were parked in front of the crib. They all had front tags with the letters YBM or SB. *What is this about?*

As Teco went up to the door, he took a deep breath before knocking. He stepped inside of a house full of people in fly gear. Big jewels flashed over the entire room.

Bashi came up to Teco and put his arm around him and said, "This is all for you."

The SB Crew was really quiet at the sight of Teco. Bashi cleared his throat and said, "Let's get this thing started, because we need to hit the road." Bashi instructed Teco to take a seat. The YBM Crew stood up and introduced themselves to Teco.

"Nice to meet you, I'm Yusef."

"Wassup? I'm Rasheed."

"I'm Basil."

"I'm the boss, Lil' Tim; and these are the men that make this all happen."

No one in the Crew was older than 26-years-old. Their goal was to make serious money. They sat at the table going through two hours of schooling Teco on *The 10 SB Rules of Honor*, which were:

1. *Everything is strictly business; and nothing is personal.*
2. *We are family and not friends.*
3. *No drug selling at the crib.*
4. *You stay or lay.*
5. *No drug dealing outside of the family.*
6. *SB members can't be considered a YBM member, can't mix with YBM affairs, can't stop over to YBM's headquarters.*
7. *All SB members are to live in the SB Crib.*
8. *SB members are to respect the ranks.*
9. *Follow all commands as given.*
10. *Put to sleep anyone who violates any SB codes which would cause a member to be in any danger for his or her life; and no one is to be put down unless the whole family agrees.*

Then they presented Teco with his own ring with SB engraved on it. GQ looked at him with hatred. She didn't want Teco in the Crew; however, she had nothing to say about it either. Teco put the ring on his right hand and smiled as he shook everyone's hand. Then, Bashi gave Teco an envelope with 5 gees. "This is your pocket money to buy some gear, when we get to Atlantic City."

Teco accepted the money and put it in his pockets. They all headed towards the door laughing and smiling. Teco rode in the car with Rasheed, who told Teco about how he was brought into YBM. "It was a lot harder back then. We were just starting the Crew and didn't have the kind of loot we have today."

Within one hour, they reached Atlantic City and drove past all the big time gambling casinos. At one point, Teco thought they were in Las Vegas.

"I didn't know that the casinos were out here," said Teco.

"Yeah man, some of the shops we're goin' to are in the casino hotels."

They pulled up to the hotel. "Welcome to Bally's sir," said the bellhop, who valet parked the car. Rasheed gave him a $100 tip.

Teco saw this and asked, "Does it cost that much to park here?"

"No, but if you playin' big, you must spend big."

Even in the day time, the casino lights shined to let you know that you are in the mist of money and a fine casino.

The first place they went to was the Gucci shop. "Remember, you have 5 gees to spend," said Bashi.

Teco came to a rack full of Gucci sweatsuits. He picked out one with a $1500 tag. His eyes got very big; and under his breath, Teco said, "Shiiit, I'm not buyin' that."

Bashi came beside him and said, "Look, you only live once. If you like it, buy it."

By the time he arrived at the third store, Teco was broke. Bashi gave him another stack of money, and said, "Yo, get what you like. This is your day."

The entire Crew bought clothes, shoes, sneakers, hats, and more jewels. Teco felt like a million dollar playa. Deep in his head, he knew it was something to this shopping spree. Whatever it was, he was ready for it at any time. On the way back to Philly, Bashi and GQ filled Teco in on more rules. Once close to the crib, they stopped at a local mall to get some street gear to wear on the block.

Back at the crib, he took all of his things out of the car. GQ showed Teco to his room upstairs. Teco looked at the shopping bags. *"Yes! Yes! I'm the shit now."*

Bashi came into Teco's room and asked, "Yo, we're going to Ivy Hill tonight. You rollin' wit us?"

"Yeah, I'll be ready." Then Teco called both Fatboy and Me-Me and asked them each to meet him at the bar.

When Teco came back downstairs he said, "Bashi, I need to get my hair cut. I'll be right back."

"Okay, just be careful. As a matter of fact, take my car." Bashi threw Teco the keys; and GQ didn't like that at all.

"You hardly ever let me drive," said GQ.

"That's because you think you are Evel Knievel," replied Bashi.

Later that evening, the SB Crew was dressed to kill. This was the second time Teco saw Cap with the Crew. They went to the bar; and Teco couldn't believe how the employees treated them like Stars.

When Fatboy entered the bar, he was looking for Teco everywhere. Teco spotted Fatboy immediately. However, Fatboy never looked for him to be with the SB Crew. So Teco got up to greet his best friend.

"Yo, wassup homey?" Teco asked while displaying his ring in front of Fatboy.

"Yo, wassup, Teco? Where you been?"

"Sittin' in the cut with the Crew."

"What Crew?"

"SB, you know how it goes."

"Can you get me in?" asked Fatboy.

Teco grabbed Fatboy on the shoulder. "I'll see. Let's drink." Teco had no intentions of bringing Fatboy into the Crew. Never let your right hand know what your left hand is doing.

The only people, who were allowed in the VIP section, were the Crew and women. Teco overhead Bashi say, "Yo, Yo, look ova there." This fine skimmie was coming through the door. As she got closer, Teco could see that it was Me-Me.

"Yo chill, that's mine," said Teco.

Teco stood up; and when Me-Me saw him, a big smile came over her face. Teco took her hand and led her to the half moon table bench in the VIP section.

"These are my boyz," said Teco.

"Do they work for the Rental Car Company too?" asked Me-Me.

"No, they don't. They are the company. I'll talk to you later 'bout that."

"You don't have to. I knew you hustled all along."

"Me-Me, let's dance."

Bashi was dancing with this fine redbone skimmie next to Teco. Unexpectedly, a guy, who looked like a personal trainer, came through the crowd towards Bashi and exclaimed, "Hey Pussy! That's my woman you dancin' wit." Everyone in the bar could tell that this dude was drunk.

Bashi went for his gun. Before Bashi could pull the gun out, Teco hit the dude from the blind side, knocking him to the floor. Teco kicked him until the dude was shaking.

Bashi pulled Teco off and exclaimed, "Let's go. That's enough!" They left the dude in a puddle of blood. Teco grabbed Me-Me's hand

and led her out the door with him. Bashi grabbed the fine redbone skimmie's hand. Together they all went to the car. The police drove past them with the sirens blaring. Teco looked out the window. *That's all I need.*

Back at the SB Crib, Teco asked the redbone, "Yo, wassup wit that punk?"

"That was my old boyfriend."

"He almost got his pussy ass killed."

Teco saw Bashi waving him to come into the kitchen. "Yo, wassup Bashi?"

"Don't ever talk like that in front of women," said Bashi.

"My fault, but that punk tried you."

"Yes I know. Thanks for being there."

"Anytime." Little did Teco know that GQ was listening to their conversation from the basement door.

"We'll talk 'bout this later. For now, let's go have fun with these skimmies," said Bashi.

"I'm wit that. Can I smoke weed in the crib?"

"In your room only."

After Teco took Me-Me home and returned to the crib, Bashi, GQ, and Cap were sitting in the living room waiting for him. They talked about what went down at the bar.

Bashi said, "Man, you were on point. You almost stomped that pussy to sleep. Well, we never work the block on weekends. You done good. Enjoy the weekend doing whateva."

Teco went around to Fatboy's crib to chill with his homey, but Fatboy wasn't there. Teco decided to go downtown to Center City. He had $500 in his pocket to play with and wanted to buy Rhonda something nice.

After getting her a gift, he went to Rhonda's crib for the rest of the weekend. She was excited to see him when he walked through the door. Rhonda ran up to Teco, put her arms around his neck, and said, "Hey Baby, it's on."

CHAPTER 11

T he first day on the block for Teco was something else. As the dope fiends stood at the top of the hill in Conshohocken, Teco could see how the fiends waited for GQ and Cap to come with their breakfast. On this day, Bashi was going to show Teco a different side of the street life, in which Teco knew nothing and was about to go to school.

"See all those people?" asked Bashi.

"Yeah, I see them."

"Those are your clients, or betta said, your bread and butta."

Teco noticed that, even though GQ and Cap were known drug dealers, the people in the hood spoke to them with respect. GQ and Cap divided up the work between these two dope fiends. Then the four of them walked down the hill to start the day. Bashi took Teco to a crib stoop in order to better position Teco to see how things were operating. As Teco was told about this and that, he had many legitimate questions to ask Bashi.

"Do the Narcs come 'round?"

"Yeah, I'll show you where they post up. Come on. Let's take a walk 'round the block."

They went up the alley to avoid being noticed by anyone. Bashi explained to Teco that this little area was nothing but hills. As they stood on the corner of a one-way street called Ventor, Bashi and Teco were looking down to the small park.

"Look past those houses to the railroad tracks. That's where the Narcs post up to watch the block," said Bashi.

When the SB Crew initially arrived in Conshohocken, they came down the back roads, which were along the countryside. Bashi and Teco walked to the pizza shop, where Bashi showed him another route out of town. Then the two of them walked up Main Street to the corner where GQ and Cap were posted.

"I'll see you homies later, Strictly Business. Teco, you just watch and learn for today. Peace out," said Bashi, who turned going up the hill towards the neighborhood bar.

Teco continued to observe GQ and Cap exchange dope and money, hand to hand, until the Crew went to the pizza shop to eat lunch. "Teco go get me some soda pop," demanded GQ, who was the boss when Bashi wasn't around. Teco never liked taking orders from GQ.

At first, Teco looked at GQ as if she were crazy. Then Teco bought the soda and said, "This is yo last time tellin' me to get somethin' like this for you. If it's not related to SB's business, you get it yo'self. Whatcha think I'm a do boy."

"You could at least sho some respect for a SB sista," said GQ.

"When you on the block, you just like us, a gangsta," said Teco.

Then Teco walked from the pizza shop to the park, where he just watched the fiends sell dope. While Teco sat on a bench, he saw that this was the spot where everybody chilled. *"There are some nice lookin' women here."*

He watched the fiends sell the rest of the dope until 8pm, which made for a twelve hour day. Then the Crew called a taxi to get to the SB crib, where Teco watched as Bashi counted the money and gave GQ and Cap their cut. That night Teco didn't receive any pay, because handouts were over. In order for Teco to get his, he needed to get on the block. He wanted his share for sure and decided not to waste any time putting in the necessary work.

The next day the Crew was on the block at 7:30am. Teco didn't have anyone to sell for him, which meant that he had to go hand and hand for himself. At first working solo wasn't cool. However, after 2 to 3 hours working the block, he started reveling in the power. The fiends never told Teco about the Narcs, who were watching nearby. Teco just happened to look in that direction and saw them. He knew that he had to quickly find someone to sell his dope.

Out of no where, this skimmie came from behind Teco with the sexist voice and asked, "Hey, wassup?"

Teco turned around, with a sweeping look up and down, and asked, "Damn baby, where did you come from with your fine ass? What's yo name?"

"I'm Jernice, what's yours?"

"Teco."

"Are you working?"

He was shocked by her question. Looking at Jernice, you wouldn't know that she snorts cocaine. She looked like a cover girl for a cosmetics line. Jernice's father was black and her mother was white. Teco recalled the girls on the block hating on Jernice because of her "good hair." She had firm legs like a professional gymnast. Teco calculated in his mind that her tits were just the right size to fit into his mouth. Her waist was small which made her ass look big.

"Yeah, what do you need?" asked Teco.

"Are you working with GQ and Cap?"

"Yeah, we have the same shit."

"Well, gimme two green bags for $40."

After giving him the money she started to leave, but Teco said, "Hold up. Don't leave so fast."

"Let me tell you up front, brutha. I'm not a freak, if that's what you thinkin'."

"Now why would you think that 'bout me?"

"Because all you dope boyz think that all women who snort are freaks. I got it goin' on. You betta recognize."

Teco knew that all he had to do was break her down and she would be his freak; however, he played the *"I don't want to fuck you"* role. He said, "Hold up. Let's just exchange numbers for now and we'll go from there."

"My bad, I hope to see you tomorrow. Here is my home number."

"Sho nuff, I'll call you tonight."

GQ was watching Teco talk to Jernice Baker the entire time. When Teco realized this, he ignored GQ and went back to making money. On his first day, Teco sold the whole bomb, which gave him a boost that he might actually be good at this side of the street life.

Later at the SB crib, Bashi couldn't believe that Teco had hit on Jernice and actually obtained her phone number. Bashi said, "Jernice

might snort cocaine, but she is still a dimepiece, who can't be denied."
They laughed and Bashi gave Teco a high five.

Teco decided to go take a shower and chill out. After freshening up, he called Rhonda.

"Hello," said Teco.

"Hey baby, how are you doin'? Are you okay?" asked Rhonda with an excited voice.

"Yes, everything is just fine. Rhonda, I can't talk with you long, but I wanted to tell you that I'll be there this weekend."

"Baby, I'm goin' out of town wit my gurls this weekend."

"Okay, that's cool. Then I'll try and see you tomorrow."

"Please come before 10 or 11 tomorrow night."

"A'ight, see you later baby."

After hanging up, Teco reached into his pocket for Jernice's digits. He rolled a joint first, because his best mack went down during a high. After smoking a joint, he called the number on the paper. The line was busy.

◊◊◊◊◊

Teco was getting adjusted to the everyday routine as a drug dealer. Even the people from the hood of Conshohocken began to call him by name. On this particular day, Teco realized that he had not seen Jernice in a few days. Regardless, he continued to check out the other women on the block. There was this redbone skimmie, who wasn't all that cute; however, her body made up for the points she was missing. He remembered seeing her several times near the local store, because she was always flirtatious. Her red hair made her stand out on any street corner. The combination of her dreamy hazel eyes and the gap between her legs made her sexually attractive. However, she was as slim as Olive Oyl from the cartoon Popeye.

"Yo Red, wassup?" asked Teco.

"Who you callin' Red?"

"I'm talking to you."

"For yo 4-1-1 my name is not Red."

"Well, what is yo name?"

"That's for me to know and for you to find out." Then she laughed and walked away. Teco didn't have time to play games. He laughed, because he knew that he would be at her later.

While Teco, GQ, and Cap were chilling at the park, the Narcs rolled up on the block. Everybody started running like crazy and hit the playground fence, which ended up on a back street. Teco heard someone calling his name. As he turned to see who it was, Cap asked. "Yo, who that callin' you Teco?"

"I think that's Jernice." About a block away, there stood Jernice motioning her hand for Teco to come in her direction. "Yo, I'll catch you guys later," said Teco as he jetted.

Once beside her, he could tell by her eyes that she hadn't gotten much sleep. "Yo wassup girl?"

"Nothin', just recouping from last night. I live here with my uncle in this crib; and I was just goin' in."

"Was it that nice of a night?" Teco noticed two police cars slowly driving down the street. "Yo, let me come inside yo crib. I need to get off the streets."

"I don't know 'bout that. My uncle doesn't like for me to have people ova."

As they looked closer, the second police car came to a complete stop. "Oh shit, you gotta let me in. I'm dirty."

"Come in, but don't tell anyone."

Once inside, Teco went immediately to the living room window to see what the cop was doing. Jernice walked up behind Teco and put her hands gently on his waist. While looking out the window over his shoulder, she asked, "Why haven't you called me? I knew you were full of shit."

Teco turned around. Now face to face with Jernice, he said, "First of all, you betta learn how to talk to me 'cause no woman in her right mind would speak to me like that."

Jernice took a step back. "My fault. When I first met you, I was really likin' yo style."

"Oh, so you tellin' me that you don't like my style anymore?"

"Yeah, I like you; but you act as though I'm a waste of yo time."

"No, it's not like that. When you gave me yo number, I did call you; but the line was busy."

"See, if you would have called back, we could have gotten to know each other by now."

"So, wassup now?"

"Oh, you think I'm that easy? Well, to tell you the truth I was thinkin' that we could smoke some weed and snort some powder."

"Why do you snort?"

"I have fun when I snort. Do you like to have fun?"

"What type of fun are you talkin' 'bout?"

"If you gimme a treat, I'll let you lick some powder off my nipples. Would you like that?"

"Hell yeah, let's get naked."

"First, you have to gimme my treat." She knew she had him right where she wanted him, because she could see that his wood was hard in his pants.

Teco said, "Here is 1 red bag for covering my ass. Here are 4 green bags for yo entertainment pleasure."

Jernice started pulling off his clothes; and Teco said, "Ooh, I like the way you play." Then Teco pulled off her clothes. As she snorted, Teco had her bending over the couch.

"Teco! You black muthafucka. Fuck this pussy, baby. Yes. Yes." He had her on her toes, grabbed her by the waist, and pulled her closer to him. Her legs began to shake. Jernice wanted him to go faster, but Teco pulled out of her.

She begged him, "No baby, please don't stop. Put it back in."

He sat in the chair and told her to climb on top of him. After she eased down, she started going faster; however, Teco said in a soft spoken voice, "No, no, come closer to me and slow down. Take your time." Then she let out a long amorous moan. He pulled her even closer by palming her ass. As he shifted to the edge of the chair, the head of his wood hit her G-spot. After three hard strokes she gripped down on his shoulder and said, "Ooh, ooh, Teco you're makin' me shake again. Yes. Yes. I love the way you throw this dick." As she talked to him, she was popping that pussy trying to get all she could from him. Then her eyes started to tear because it felt so good to her.

"Are you alright?" asked Teco.

"Yes, it's just that I've never had anyone take me there like you."

As their rhythm came to a natural end, Teco asked, "Where can I clean myself?"

"The bathroom is on the left down the hall."

Teco picked up his clothes and went to take a shower. As he came out of the bathroom, Jernice was standing by the door. He said, "I think it's time for me to push on."

"Are you just gonna leave?"

Teco didn't respond, because he knew he had to keep her in check by not having sex with her all of the time.

"Teco, you know I got to have more of that good sex."

"Yeah, we'll see how you act," said Teco nonchalantly.

"Will I see you again?"

CHAPTER 12

Teco left to see what was happening on the block. As he turned the corner, things seemed to be back to normal. Even though he didn't see the rest of the Crew, he started doing business again. He was grinding his ass off, running from car to car. Before he knew it, he was sold out. GQ and Cap turned the corner as Teco was walking away from a car.

"Yo, how long you been out here?" asked Cap.

"For 'bout 2 hours," replied Teco.

"So what happened to the Narcs?"

"How in the hell should I know? Ask those crackheads."

After getting a soda, Teco went to the park and watched the block. From where he was seated, he could see that everything was going well. That's when he remembered he had to be back at SB to check in his stash.

When the Crew returned to the SB crib, Bashi counted the money. Teco was hoping that Bashi didn't see the panic in his eyes. *"How did I let Jernice sucker me out of 5 bags? Bashi is gonna be buggin'."*

Bashi exclaimed, "GQ and Cap, that's what I'm talkin' 'bout! . . . Ok Teco, lay it out on the table." Teco began to think about what he was going to tell Bashi. Beads of sweat started forming on his brow. If he told Bashi that his personal life interfered with business, Bashi would have his ass put to sleep for stealing, because those are the rules. Teco also knew that he couldn't tell a lie. Trust means everything to business men like Bashi. *"Think. Think. Think . . ."*

"Teco. Teco. Are you listenin'?" asked Bashi in a frustrated voice.

"Yo, Yo, wassup up? Wassup up?"

"Why is it only $1,900 here?"

"See, I gave 2 green and 1 red to my runner for watchin' my back after the Narcs left. Then when I was ova Jernice's crib, I gave her 2 green bags for lettin' me freak her."

As he said that, everyone in the room looked up in amazement. Teco didn't know if they were buying his story about the bags; so he didn't say a word.

Cap questioned, "You did what to Jernice?"

"Jernice and me got naked and freaked for 'bout one hour in her livin' room. I got that on lock."

The room was silent for what Teco thought was an eternity. Then Bashi exclaimed, "DAMN!" Bashi and Cap laughed and gave Teco a high five.

GQ gave Teco a cold look and said, "Men."

Then Bashi broke Teco off well; and Teco said, "Thanks man. I need to call my girl Rhonda. I'll check you later."

Teco tried to call Rhonda, but for some strange reason her phone was disconnected. He then called her job; and she picked up the phone. "Thank you for calling Comfort Inn. This is Rhonda. May I help you?"

"Yo, wassup wit yo phone?"

"I had the number changed."

"Why didn't you tell me you had—"

"Look, I don't have time to play games wit you as you run the streets. You can come get yo shit and yo money."

"No, what you do is bring it to work with you tomorrow; and I'll pick it up then."

"Why can't you pick it up from my house?"

"Because I don't have time to play yo games. You know if I come to the crib, we will probably have sex and blah, blah, blah. I'm not for that shit. Bring my things to work wit you." There was silence. "See you tomorrow." Teco said and hung up.

◊◊◊◊◊

Teco was so good at getting new clientele, that the people around Conshohocken no longer gave Teco mad respect. In fact, this dude named Bubbles, who was the owner of the neighborhood bar, really didn't care for anyone from the SB Crew, especially Bashi. Recently Bubbles' woman, Shardonnay, was buying powder from Teco. This ticked Bubbles off. Plus, Shardonnay talked too much about how she liked the way Teco handled business. Bubbles finally had enough when he overheard Shardonnay telling a female customer that Teco was so fine. In his mind, Bubbles could still hear the tone of his woman's voice when she talked about Teco. *"Gurl, I wish I could get in them pants."* Bubbles was sick of it.

Teco was in the back pool room, when two fiends walked in the bar. They joined Teco to buy some dope. As soon as Bubbles saw the two fiends leave, he approached Teco with an evil look and whispered underneath his breath, "Teco, don't sell dope in my bar. And don't mess wit my woman. Let this be the last time I tell you." Then Bubbles took a pool stick and broke it in half.

Teco looked at him with a challenging stare. "Yeah, whateva man. Just chill." Being in the bar was one way Teco stayed out of sight; and he needed this spot. In spite of Bubbles' reaction, Teco finished a round of pool.

After walking down the hill to check out the scene, he couldn't believe what he saw. Right before his eyes, the cops had set up a roadblock, stopping every car. Teco had to find a place to go. He saw this old lady sitting outside of her home and knew she would be a great cover.

"Excuse me ma'am. Do you mind if I sit here wit you for a moment?"

"I don't like what you boys do; but I won't let those police get you either. Sure have a seat, son." Her long grey hair was pulled back into a pony tail. Teco noticed the veins and age spots on the back of her hands. She continued to say, "Young man, if you keep doin' these thangs you doin', you ain't gonna live to see 30. Sometimes no one has to kill ya, 'cause ya end up killin' yo'self. Ya can't take money to the grave wit ya. You need God. You ever thought 'bout gettin' sa—"

The door swung open. As Teco turned, a big smile came over his face. His redbone friend appeared and asked, "Nana, is this boy botherin' you?"

"Oh no baby. He's a nice young man. He just needs to quit doin' his wrong."

"Have you found out my name yet?" The redbone asked Teco.

"No, I was hopin' you would tell me."

"Nope, it won't be that easy either; besides, I'm leaving now." Teco saw that she had a habit of just walking away in the middle of conversations.

Her grandmother leaned forward in her chair and said, "Her name is Cassandra."

◊◊◊◊◊

After the heat was off, the Crew met up at the park to discuss what had just happened.

"Yeah, they just busted the store for selling weed," said GQ.

"So how does this affect us?" asked Teco.

"I don't know yet," said GQ.

"Do you think we should leave?" asked Cap.

"Well, it's only 6pm," said Teco.

"We have two more hours; so let's post up in the crib on the back street," said GQ. Bashi had a specific crib for the fiends to come and buy dope.

This female, Crazy Pat, came over to sell Valiums to GQ, who liked getting fucked up. Teco didn't know anything about Valiums or this aspect of the street life. However, he was following GQ's lead. Crazy Pat had fives and tens. Teco bartered 5 pills for 1 red bag. He immediately took 2 Vees and chased it down with beer. Within 20 minutes, Teco was looking for the high, but didn't know what to expect. *"Man, I don't feel nothin'."*

It was time for the Crew to leave and go back to the SB crib. As they drove home, a police car pulled behind them. Just as Teco made a right turn headed toward Philly, the blue and red lights started to flash.

"Teco, pull ova. He's just messing wit us," said Cap.

Teco's first instinct was to punch the gas peddle. Instead, he pulled over and rolled down the window. Just as the outside air hit him, the Vees took over; and he felt very relaxed. An officer came to the driver's door and said, "License and registration please."

"I left my license at home in my other jacket. The registration is in the glove box; let me get it . . ."

"No need. Step out of the car."

As Teco opened the door, he realized that the weed he had in his jacket pocket was missing. Somehow, two bags fell onto the ground. The cop never saw the weed, because the cop was too busy looking at GQ and Cap. With a swift motion, Teco scooped up the weed and put it back into his pocket.

◊◊◊◊◊

"Come in," said Bashi

"Man, what happened?" asked Teco. The last thing Teco remembered was standing beside the car; but when he woke up, he was in his bed at the SB Crib.

"You took too many of those Vees. You betta leave that shit alone."

"Yeah, you right. Can I use yo car? I need to pick up my things from Rhonda."

"Ummm. Leave that stuff alone too." Bashi laughed and threw Teco the keys to his Jetta.

When Teco got to Rhonda's job, he was feeling really nice, because he had smoked a sizeable joint on the way. Rhonda was at the front desk. Teco said, "Hello Rhonda. You lookin tight."

"Thank You. You don't look bad yo'self."

As he looked into her eyes, she had an exotic expression on her face. He was waiting for her to make her move.

She reached into the desk drawer and said, "Baby, take this key. Yo things are in Room 143. I'll be there to speak with you in 20 minutes."

"Hell no. We both know my things are not in that room. I didn't come for no pussy."

"If you want your clothes and money, I think you should be a little, let's say, open to my way."

Teco really wanted to hit that once more just to let her know what she would be missing. So he decided to flip the script. Teco said in a deep sexy voice, "Why be formal, if you want it yo way, just bend ova right here. You love it from the back. Are you wet and ready?"

"Teco, not here. Please, just take the key and go. I promise it will be worth yo while. I miss my Ching Chong Stick."

"Oh so, now it's yours." Teco reached for the keys and gave her a passionate kiss. "Don't keep me waitin'."

Teco was sitting on the couch completely naked when Rhonda arrived in the room. She stood there astonished. "So you think you can make my Kitty Kat meow and convince me to fall back in love with yo fine ass, only to leave me again?"

"Don't start. You the one who called it off. I was gonna spend the entire weekend hittin' yo G-spot, remember? You went to see your gurls or so you say."

"Hell, you sexed me up for weeks before you went to live with the SB Crew. Then you left me horny wantin' you. What do you expect? I just can't be sittin' 'round waitin' for you to call. Now gimme some of my Ching Chong Stick for the last time. That's all I need to make this ache go away."

"So now you just want me to hit it and run? What sense does that make? You trippin'."

"And don't think that you are gonna gimme a quickie. I want it nice and slooow, just like you like it."

Teco made sure Rhonda was satisfied throughout the entire night. At sunrise, Teco decided he should check-in with Bashi to let him know what was up. During the conversation, Bashi said, "I need a couple of rooms for a party. Ask Rhonda to hook us up."

"Rhonda, my peeps want to get a room next week. Can you hook a brutha up?"

"Yeah, only if you take care of my Kitty Kat some more."

"Yo Bashi, I'll talk to you when I get in." Teco hung up the phone, looked at Rhonda, and asked, "So you want to pimp me now?"

"No, just see that I get mine."

"Well, all future stays for me and my boyz are free, 'cause I'm not cheap."

She laughed at him and rose up from the bed. "So what are you gonna do wit yo clothes?"

"What the hell you think I'm gonna do? I'm takin' my shit wit me."

She reached into her purse and pulled out a Crown Royal bag. "Here's yo money. It's all there. Get yo clothes from the trunk of my car."

They showered and got dress. As they left the room headed towards the parking lot, Teco smacked her on the ass. She smiled and said, "I see you still like this ass."

Teco transferred his clothes to Bashi's car. As he opened the car door to leave, Rhonda said, "When you're ready to get those rooms, call me. Then we can work somethin' out wit my Ching Chong stick."

CHAPTER 13

This started off as a bad day for Teco. He lost an ounce of weed, which really pissed him off big time. Every day before he hit the block, he would smoke a joint, but not this morning.

Teco had his mind on some real different shit today. As he sat on his bed, he looked over at a baseball bat and two metal lighters. He got up, went to the kitchen, pulled open the tool drawer, and got the black electrical tape. After returning to his room, he tightly taped a lighter to each side of the bat. Then he covered the entire bat with the black tape. Teco swung the bat as if he were taking someone's head off. *"Yeah, this is my new Pay Me Stick."*

As they hit the block, each of the Crew members went separate ways. Teco went to the bar; however, it was closed. So instead, he headed to the park to chill. For some reason, the block wasn't busy today. As he sat on the park bench, he knew that selling dope wasn't his style of making money. He never liked looking over his shoulders all the time. Plus he was in an area in which he knew little. He missed his Johnnies.

While he was at the park, Cassandra came down the street. Teco knew that his love of sex was his biggest distraction.

"Wassup Cassandra?"

When he said her name, she looked at him in total shock. Cassandra said, "Be sittin' right there when I come back from the store."

She returned, sat next to him on the bench, and put her arm around his shoulders. "You slow. It's 'bout time you know my name."

"I've known yo name for some time. I was just waitin' for the right time to say it. Like now."

"I've been likin' you for a good while." Teco had a confused look on his face. She said, "Don't act. You know what time it is."

"What are you tryin' to tell me?" Teco knew what was up and what was on her mind. Why was she relinquishing control so soon? She didn't know him. Teco continued to say, "Well to be honest, you do have a sexy gap."

"That's all you see? You dope boyz are all the same. Later."

GQ walked up to Teco and said, "Yo, I'll be right back. I need to take a quick drive up to Norristown. So gimme the keys to the ride." Teco gave her the keys and went into the store.

The store owner pointed to Teco and said, "You! I see you sellin' drugs. If you come in here, please don't bring any wit you. I can't afford to get hit again."

◊◊◊◊◊

Once GQ reached Norristown, she stopped at Travis' crib. Travis stayed in and out of jail for petty crimes and was a local nobody. GQ and Travis grew up in the same hood and still kicked it every now and then. She rang the doorbell to his apartment; and Travis opened the door wearing only Calvin Klein white boxers. He was glad to see GQ and invited her inside.

Travis Dagatto towered over GQ; but when he reached down to kiss her, the moment carried her away from the streets into a world of complete bliss. After he released her, Travis looked into her hazel eyes. A glimpse into her eyes allured men to tell secrets to her in which they never shared with their wives.

GQ loved the way he fingered his curly black hair out of his face and how he smiled as if there were not a care in the world. He was the only man who made GQ feel whole. As she reached up to embrace him, Travis lifted her up off of the floor in order for her to feel that his wood was hard. He couldn't wait to make love to her all night long.

"Travis, Travis, I'm not here for sex. I'm here on business." She said as she noticed that his tanned skin was smooth and clear.

"Come on Gail. I just got out of jail; and I haven't had any for months. Let me just hit it from the back. Afterwards, I promise you can get on top like you like it." Travis eased her feet back onto the floor and started to suck on her neck, giving her a hicky. Then he eased his hand under her sweat shirt.

"Baby, Baby, we need to talk 'bout our future," said GQ.

"That can wait 'til the mornin'. Let me take your sweats off and kiss your tits. Betta yet, let me put my finger in your hot pussy to feel how wet you are from waitin' on your man to come home," said Travis as the sunlight in the room made her eyes look the color of light-blue.

"Travis, focus on us . . . together . . . set for life."

The phrase "set for life" caught his attention. He removed his hand from under her sweat shirt, looked into her now almond-blue eyes, and said, "Okay, I'm listenin' Gail."

"Look baby, I need you on the streets. There is this punk ass bum named Teco who Bashi brought on wit the Crew. Teco is tryin' to take my spot. I need you to work wit me."

"Gail, you know you can whoop his ass by yo'self."

"I ain't talkin' 'bout no school yard shit."

"So, what you talkin' 'bout?" asked Travis.

"I'm ready to run my own crew. I just need to move some people out my way. You dig?"

"Yeah, I can dig what you sayin'."

"So, you in?"

"Yeah, I'm in."

"Okay baby, I gotta—"

"Gail come on. I had to look at crusty ass dudes for 6 long months in county. Don't leave me now. Baby I love you. Gimme some of that cat girl lovin' with those exquisite eyes."

GQ reached up and softly touched his lips with her thumb and said, "I missed you too; but I gotta get back to the block before Cap and Teco start buggin'. Our future depends on me being on point. I'll be back tonight. I promise. Don't start without me." Then GQ placed Travis' hand on her butt and gave him an erotic kiss.

As GQ walked out of the house, Travis watched her fine phatt ass. He went to the window and imagined her sexy legs easing into the car. *"Why she always coverin' up those hot legs? Uh, Uh, Uh, now I gotta go take a shower."*

◊◊◊◊◊

Teco wanted something out of the store; however, he knew he couldn't take his product into the store. He found a hole in the bottom of the wall. Teco looked around carefully to see if anyone was watching him. There was no one around, or so he thought. He put his stash in the hole and covered it with some trash that he found on the ground.

After making his purchase, he returned to the spot. "Oh Shit!" An elderly man passed by with a disapproving look about Teco's language. "Pardon me sir." Teco said. Teco searched different areas of the wall and on the ground. *"Who the fuck took my shit?"*

He looked once more to be sure that he wasn't trippin'. When he rose up off his knees, he looked all around. No one was in sight. Teco was mad as hell and could have killed someone. He went back into the store to tell GQ and Cap.

"Go call Bashi and let him know what happened," said Cap.

Teco went to the pay phone by the pizza shop to make the call. The phone rang six times. "Yo, wassup?" asked Bashi.

"Bashi, this is Teco. I have some bad news."

"What happened?"

"Somebody took my bomb."

"What! What the hell do you mean?!" Bashi yelled.

"Man, the store dude wouldn't let me come in wit my stash. So I had to hide it. When I came out, it was gone."

"Just stay down there, until it's time to come home. I'll speak to you later 'bout this."

Teco went back to the block watching everyone's move. Cassandra approached him and said, "So wassup? Are you coming wit me or what?"

"No! Right now isn't a good time."

"Damn Teco, what the hell is wrong wit you?"

"Somebody just stole my bomb. So, I'll get up wit you some other day."

"Okay, I'll be waitin' for you," said Cassandra.

Teco didn't want to hear what Bashi had to say. This was a major fuck up for him. He knew that somebody had to pay for his bomb being stolen. *"Who had seen me put it there?"*

On the way to the crib, GQ snapped on Teco for letting someone steal his bomb. "How in the hell did you let someone take our shit?" The tone of her voice was making Teco vexed.

"Bitch, I thought nobody had seen me."

"Who you callin' a bitch? In this line of work, somebody is always watchin' yo ass," said GQ.

Teco wanted to deal with this pooh butt bitch for trying to check him. Given the chance, Teco was going to take her position in SB. Teco knew GQ didn't want him in the Crew, because she treated him as a threat to her authority. She wasn't one to be coy, but Teco wasn't sure if GQ would hone in on her feminine traits to keep her position. He decided then and there to keep a close eye on her.

When they walked into the crib, Bashi said, "Just tell me what the fuck happened."

GQ started to explain. "See Teco couldn't go into the store with his stash—"

"I know that. Why were all of you in the store at the same time?" asked Bashi. GQ, Cap, and Teco looked at each other. Bashi continued to say, "Somebody should have been on the block at all times makin' my fuckin' money!"

"We were takin' a break," said GQ.

"All of you at one time? Hell NO! Someone should have been out there. Plus, why aren't you watchin' each other's backs?" asked Bashi.

Teco tried to give some form of explanation, but Bashi wasn't giving anyone an opportunity to speak.

"This is the deal. All of you will pay for that bomb. You leave as a Crew, come back as a Crew, and you suffer as a Crew. It's just like that. Now lay it out on the table," demanded Bashi.

They all pulled out the money for the day and compensated Bashi for the loss. GQ and Cap both looked at Teco with sheer anger.

Then Bashi pulled Teco to the side. "Teco come wit me to my office and let me speak with you alone." Teco sat down not knowing which lecture to expect. "I want you to understand that in this business, you must learn to take a loss. When one teammate is careless, the entire Crew suffers. Listen, I did some checking around. I know who took your bomb." Bashi could see revenge written on Teco's face. "One of the fiends, Bobby took your bomb. But let it go. That will be all for now. You are free to leave."

"I'm gonna kill that bitch ass fiend."

The next morning, the Crew left the crib without exchanging words. Teco's mind was on beating the shit out of Bobby. As soon as Teco hit the block, he saw Bobby, who had a wrestler's body frame and broad shoulders. Many people around the area were afraid of Bobby.

Bobby walked up to Teco and said, "Let me get a red bag." As Bobby reached into his pocket for the money, Teco struck Bobby with a Mike Tyson blow. Bobby fell to the ground. Teco kicked him in the face and ribs. You could hear Bobby's screams from up the street.

"I bet you won't take nobody else's shit. Will you? Say you sorry. Say you sorry, you fuckin' dope head bitch!" exclaimed Teco.

Bobby was unconscious and couldn't reply. Because GQ was strong for her size, she was able to pull Teco off of Bobby. GQ asked Teco, "What the fuck are you tryin' to do? Commit a homicide?"

When Teco stopped, he had blood all over his sneakers.

"Man, you need to go clean yo'self off," said GQ.

As Teco left, he heard the ambulance coming down the street. He had to leave the block; therefore, he went to the SB Crib. On the way to the crib, Teco keep repeating, *"He took my shit. If I had to pay; then he had to pay."*

As Teco approached the front door, Bashi came out and asked, "Didn't I tell you to leave it alone?"

"Man, how you find out so fast? If I stole from you, there is no way that you would just let me come back and buy more dope from you."

"GQ told me that you almost killed that dude. Are you tryin' to catch a body? Yo new name is Homicide because you real dangerous. I like yo style. You don't take no shit and I need that on my team; but you need to control yo temper."

"Man, let me go clean off."

The hot water from the shower relaxed every muscle in Teco's body. *"Homicide. Homicide. Yeah, that fits me."* After getting out of the shower Teco looked in the mirror, reached for the clippers, and shaved his head bald. *"With the new name, comes a new look."*

He put on a Gucci sweatsuit. Then he walked to the mall. The first place, he stopped was the jewelry shop. He walked to the glass case to look at all the different pieces. The man behind the counter came up to Teco, a.k.a. Homicide, and asked, "Yes sir, may I help you?"

"Yes, I would like to have a three finger ring made."

"What style would you like sir?"

"May I see that one?" Homicide asked pointing to a nice ring.

"Sure." As Homicide had the ring in this hand, he checked it out closely.

"This one will be fine. I want HSB in diamonds put on it."

"To have real stones put on it will cost $800."

"How long will it take to make?"

"Just gimme 2 hours sir."

"Okay, that will be cool."

"Sir, you need to pay the entire $800 now."

"No, I'll pay half now." *"These jewelers think they are so damn slick."* Homicide didn't trust anyone but Bashi.

He left the store and went to the Eye Wear Shop. He knew exactly what type of shades he wanted for his new look.

"May I see these Alpina sunglasses please?"

"Yes, this is our last pair on sale for $1000. It comes with a warranty."

"Are they real gold?"

"Yes, 14k"

Homicide tried them on and looked into the counter mirror. *"These chumpies are hot and fit me right."*

"I'll take them."

He knew he was the shit. Everybody who was about something had these shades, because they stood out from a distance.

After paying for his shades, he went to Gerrets Lounge. He hadn't been there since the Aaron ordeal. As soon as he stepped inside, the waitress came up to him and asked, "Would you like a seat at a table?"

"Yes, that's cool." She walked him to a round table and gave him a menu. "I would like a Heineken to start wit."

He was even happier that his new shades had indoor/outdoor lens. Homicide was feeling exceptional now that he had his own money. The only thing he needed was a car to make his role complete.

When the waitress came back, she said, "I like yo glasses."

"Thank you. Can I have a regular Philly Cheesesteak wit onion rings?"

"Will that be all?"

"No, I need an ounce of weed."

"Are you the po po?"

"Hell no."

"Well, wait here."

CHAPTER 14

As Homicide drank his beer, he noticed this dude with curly black hair watching him, which pissed Homicide off. Then the waitress came back and put a tray on the table. "That will be $75."

Homicide knew that they had a nice system for selling their weed. He gave her $90. Once she left, he slid the reefer off of the tray into his pocket. He finished his Philly Cheesesteak and left the bar.

After Homicide picked up the ring from the jewelry store, he wanted to show Fatboy his purchases; however, Fatboy wasn't home. So he decided to go straight to the SB Crib to show Bashi his newest pieces. "Damn Homicide, that joint is nice. Look, I need you to go wit me. I'll explain it to you on the way. Let's split," said Bashi.

Bashi drove to Summerville and parked on Huntes Street. Then Bashi pulled out a heater, gave it to Homicide, and said, "Look this is the deal. These Ville boyz owe me some lute. So this is how it's goin' down. We'll walk up to that crib . . ." Bashi pointed to the crib with the blue door. ". . . When I knock on the door, this female will come to the door. When she does, I want you to kick the door in. It should be two dudes in the house wit her. I'll grab the girl. You get those dudes and lay them down on the floor. The .38 is very heavy; smack them in the head, if need be."

"What are we goin' in there to get other than yo lute?"

"Let me deal wit that. I just need you to watch my back."

"A'ight, let's do this," said Homicide.

"Wait, we need to do somethin' first."

Bashi got out of the car and opened the trunk. "Here put this on, take yo rings off, and take this ducktape wit you."

After Bashi gave Homicide a black one piece jumpsuit, bandana, and gloves, they walked down to the crib. Bashi looked through the window and saw two men sitting on the couch. One of them was bagging some weed. Bashi put up two fingers and pointed to the window. Bashi and Homicide were crouched like two creeping tigers. Bashi knocked on the door. Homicide already had the heater in his left hand.

A female came to the door and asked, "Who is it?"

Right then and there Bashi gave Homicide the signal. Homicide drew his leg back and kicked the door in with one blow. Boom!

The door went flying open and pushed the girl into the wall. Homicide rushed into the house. One guy tried to run; but Homicide caught him in the back of the head with the heater. As soon as the .38 made contact, blood splattered.

"Don't nobody move! Lay the fuck down pussy!"

No one in the house could see who Bashi and Homicide were, because of the black bandanas over their faces.

"Tie them up and put them on the couch." Homicide did as Bashi had instructed. Bashi continued to say, "Where's the money?"

"I'll give it to you man. You don't have to do this."

"Shut the fuck up and tell him where the money is," said Homicide.

Bashi brought the female into the room, put Ducktape around her mouth and pointed a 9 mm at her head. "One of you pussies betta say somethin'."

"Yo, hurry up. We don't have long," said Homicide.

The female was trying to say something. Bashi pulled the tape from her mouth, which was bleeding from her being hit by the door. "It's all in the basement."

"You know where it is?" asked Bashi.

She nodded yes. Bashi walked to the basement with the female headed in first, in case this was a trap. Once there, she stood in front of a white freezer.

"It's in there?" asked Bashi.

"Yes, at the bottom."

"You go get it out and put it in this bag." Bashi had the heater to the back of her head, to reinforce his statement. She did as he said without incident. Bashi put more tape over her mouth, told her to lie down, and taped up her hands. "You betta not move!"

Bashi went upstairs, where Homicide was waiting for the other man to make a wrong move; however, the dude was cooperating.

"Yo, let's go," said Bashi.

With his back towards the door, Homicide said, "Yo, Bashi wait in the car. I need to take care of somethin'."

As Bashi sat down in the passenger's seat of the car, all Bashi heard was Pop! Pop! Pop! Once Homicide reached the car, he quickly drove off.

"Yo, did you put them to sleep?"

"All the way."

Back at the SB crib, Homicide went into his room and looked in the mirror. *"You done lost your mind."*

Bashi came in the room to see if Homicide was alright, knowing that he had never done anything like this before. "My main man, you did real good back there. Here, this is for you." Bashi gave Homicide $6,000 and a pound of weed.

"Bashi let me get some powder to calm my nerves."

Bashi looked at Homicide as if he were crazy. Then Bashi said, "A'ight come on to my room." He gave Homicide some off of the scale in a $5 bill.

Homicide took it to his room and shut the door. *"Dope, weed, and money. I can't go wrong."* Then Homicide recalled what the CSI lady asked when Blue died. *"The street life, is it suicide or murder?"*

◊◊◊◊◊

GQ was no longer the right-hand to Bashi. Homicide had worked his way up the power chain in the SB Crew, just as GQ had predicted. Bashi now depended on Homicide for everything. Homicide no longer had to sell dope on the block, unless he wanted to make some extra dough. He became Bashi's bodyguard, watching the Crew's back with his heater. On this day, Homicide was also carrying his Pay Me Stick.

This white dude came up to Homicide and asked, "Do you want to buy a 12 gage pump for $100?"

"Let me see it first."

"Come wit me to my house." They walked two blocks to this guy's crib. Homicide kept his hand on his heater just in case this was a set up. The guy showed him the shot gun, which was a hunting pump rifle in mint condition.

"Let me go get my car and the money."

Homicide drove back to the white dude's crib and gave him $100. He wanted neither GQ nor Cap to know about the pump until the time was right. So, he put the shot gun in the trunk and made sure he parked in the same parking spot when he returned to the block.

As Homicide was walking down the hill, Cassandra walked up to him and asked, "Can I speak with you?"

"Sure, wassup?"

"When are you gonna let me get some of that?"

"Girl, you need to stop playin'. You know you can't handle this."

"Well, let's see." Cassandra had on a pair of loose shorts and a tight tank top. "Follow me." She said with a seductive smile.

They walked up to this abandoned garage. As they walked, Homicide's eyes were affixed on her sexy gap. He couldn't believe that she was so easy. She opened the door, which was on the side of the garage. He kept his hand on his heater and looked around to make sure that this wasn't a set up either. Out of the blue, Cassandra started kissing him on his neck. He responded by grabbing her on her little soft ass. As she pulled down his zipper, his wood started to rise; but he told her to stop. He removed his heater from his waist with his left hand. When she saw the gun, she asked, "Wassup wit the gun?"

"Look, don't worry 'bout the gun." He pulled down his pants with his right hand. His wood popped out. Cassandra could barely wait for him to gain his balance and started reaching for his wood. As she was stroking it from the head to his balls, Homicide couldn't understand why she was rushing things so fast. Then unexpectedly, Cassandra turned around, pulled her shorts down, and bent over. Homicide put his wood in her hot pussy. Then he began to slow stroke with his right hand on her back and his left hand on the heater. He knew that he had to be ready to cap anyone who tried to violate his space. He wanted to fuck her, but not like this. Teco, a.k.a. Homicide, hit her G-Spot from the best angle. Cassandra said, "Oh Teco. Oh Teco. I'm . . ." Cassandra let out a loud moan when she climaxed. Suddenly she moved forward, which caused his wood to come out of her. Now, Homicide was pissed; but he didn't have time to fool around with her anymore. *Women like Cassandra give women who snort a bad rep. Jernice was right.*" After this episode, he would never have respect for Cassandra again.

Homicide went to the bar to clean off before meeting back up with GQ and Cap. As he came out of the bathroom, Homicide saw GQ sitting alone at the table in the pool room.

"Let me ask you somethin'. What did Bashi and you do the other night?" asked GQ.

Homicide looked at GQ funny, wondering why she wanted to know about the other night. "Why you all up in my bus? I don't know what you talkin' 'bout. You asked Bashi?" Something was telling him to be ready to fire down on GQ, if necessary. Homicide continued to say, "I'll be back, I'm gonna watch Cap's back."

GQ thought, *"I know he did somethin' for Bashi. I need to put him under so that I can start runnin' shit again."*

Homicide walked up to Cap, who had five more bags to sell before they could call it a day. Out of no where, a red Coupe Deville Cadillac with a red top parked beside them.

"Yo, man I need some work. You dude's working," said this distinguished white man.

"Wassup? What do you need?" asked Cap.

"You got six?"

"No, only five."

"Okay, let me get that."

"Is this ride for sale?" asked Homicide.

"No, but you can rent it for a couple of bags."

"A'ight, gimme yo digits."

Because this was the last sale of the day, they left the block. Once at the crib, Homicide pulled out his leather Louis Vuitton Suit and Black Rider boots, because the SB Crew was going out to party tonight. After taking his shower, Homicide bagged up 4 ounces of weed and 20 dime bags. He put the weed in his boots, just in case he was searched.

However, he knew that the door bouncer never messed with YBM or the SB Crew.

Selling weed at the After Midnight Club was a good hustle. Tonight Steady B and DST were performing, which meant that the place would be packed. This spot was called the After Midnight Club because the doors didn't even open until midnight, yet everyone left at sunrise.

On the way to the club in Bashi's Jetta, Homicide asked Bashi to stop at the Richard Allen projects.

Homicide said, "This is a spot in Philly where you need to know someone to walk through the hood."

"What's the deal?"

"I want to show you this area because this is a future money maker for us."

As Bashi slowed down, Homicide flagged down this guy to the car.

"Yo, whatz poppin' Teco? I ain't seen you in a while."

Teco, a.k.a. Homicide, pulled out 4 ounces. "I'll be back in the mornin'. Have me $200."

As Bashi and Homicide drove off, Bashi said, "Great idea. Let's see how he moves the weed. Then we can talk 'bout future business."

They turned up the music to get in the mood for the party. The club was only three blocks away from the projects. As they waited for the club to open, they sat in the car and talked.

"Homicide, let me ask you somethin'. When did you start snorting powder?"

"I had my first line with this female named Debbie, who turned me on to it."

"Have you been using my stuff?"

CHAPTER 15

Homicide replied, "Hell no, I never used your stuff until I asked you the other night."

"Am I gonna have a problem with you and cocaine?" asked Bashi.

"No."

Bashi decided to leave the conversation alone. Homicide and Bashi saw that the line was starting to move, which indicated that it was time to party. The SB Crew knew they would get VIP treatment even though the line was a block long. When the bouncer saw Bashi, he yelled, "Yo. Yo. Back up! I said back up! Let them pass."

As the Crew pushed towards the front of the line, the female at the booth waved for them to go directly inside the club. As they went to a round table by the bar, Bashi tapped Cap on the shoulder to get his attention regarding two skimmies, who were getting their hands stamped at the door.

One skimmie was dark-skinned with a tight short hair-do. Homicide immediately noticed her nice hips and big bamboo earrings. The other skimmie was brown-skinned with a mushroom hair-do. Although she also had on bamboo earrings with a big rope chain, Homicide's eyes wandered from her large chest to her phatt ass. The dark-skinned skimmie's shirt read "Lisa" and the brown-skinned skimmie's shirt read "Sonya." Even a 12-year-old boy could tell that Lisa and Sonya wanted their names known to everyone in the club.

Bashi yelled, "Yo Lisa!" When she looked in Bashi's direction, he waved her over to the table. Lisa Turner had a way of throwing her ass in Lee jeans as she strolled across a room.

"Do I know you?" Lisa asked.

"Now you do. I'm Bashi; and this is Cap, Homicide, and our girl, GQ."

"Where are you from? asked Lisa.

"Does that matter?" asked Cap.

"Yes, because I don't fuck with South Philly boyz," said Lisa.

"Well you don't have to worry 'bout that; we're from Mt. Airy," said Homicide.

Lisa made a dramatic turn and walked back towards Sonya Styles and said, "Gurl, you need to come ova here wit me. These boyz eaten fat. I think this is that Strickly Business Crew."

"Why you think that?" asked Sonya, as she looked at the Crew.

"Because they already invitin' women to kick it with them tonight. This one girl named GQ ain't all that. She sittin' at the SB table lookin' like a pooh ass ho. Plus, these guys all have rings that say SB. The cute one's ring says HSB. His name is Homicide; so I bet his ring stands for Homicide Strictly Business."

They both walked over to the table. Lisa said, "This is my gurl Sonya."

Homicide stood up to pull out chairs for the ladies to be seated. Lisa said, "Homicide Strictly Business, what a real gentleman."

He replied, "So you think you figured out who we are. I like that."

Homicide went to the other side of the bar by the pond, where several people were smoking weed. He saw this as an opportunity to hustle; so he pulled out his stash, which went very fast. However, he kept two bags for himself.

At 5:00am, Homicide returned to the SB table. Lisa and Sonya knew how to play their cards right. They had Cap's and Bashi's full attention. GQ looked absolutely bored listening to Lisa and Sonya. Even though Homicide didn't like GQ, Homicide decided to rescue GQ from the situation and said, "Bashi, it's time to pull up." Bashi stood up from the table and gave a signal for the Crew to stand up as well.

"So Lisa, Sonya, are you two comin' wit us or what?" asked Cap.

"Yeah, if you takin' us home before noon," said Lisa.

"Yes, we can do that," said Bashi. GQ rolled her eyes.

Cap and GQ left the club with the two skimmies. Homicide drove Bashi back to Richard Allen in Bashi's Jetta. The same guy, who Homicide spoke to earlier about the 4 ounces, came running up to the car and asked, "Whatz poppin'? Is everything tight?"

Homicide asked, "So Dai Dai, how'd you do?"

"Here's $200."

Bashi looked at Dai Dai and wondered why Dai Dai's entire outfit was red. Homicide counted the lute, put it in his pocket, and said "Yo. Gimme some time. I'll see you right."

"Okay, you do that," said Dai Dai.

Homicide drove off and asked, "So boss man, what do you think 'bout Dai Dai?"

"Why does he wear red?" asked Bashi.

"You know, I asked the same thing. He said somethin' 'bout staying flamed up. Whateva that means."

"Well, before I decide how he did tonight, let's see how things run next week."

"What do you think 'bout those skimmies, Lisa and Sonya?

"I don't know, but I want Lisa," said Bashi.

"I'm not tryin' to see neither one of them, because I have somethin' to do that's very important."

"What in the hell is so important that can't wait 'til tomorrow?"

"Well, this guy sold me a pump rifle for $100. I want to saw it off tonight."

"Let me check it out when we get back to the crib."

When Homicide and Bashi parked in the driveway, GQ, Cap, and the skimmies were already in the crib. As Homicide and Bashi got out of the car, a Black SUV pulled up beside them. A pistol came out of the window; and Bashi shouted, "Homicide get down!"

They both ducked behind the Jetta. All they heard was gun fire. Pop! Pop! Pop! Pop! Pop! Neither of them had a heater. When the gun play stopped and the SUV raced away, Homicide examined himself for any signs of blood. Then he surveyed the car and saw 2 bullet holes.

Bashi asked, "Are you okay?"

"Yeah, did you get a chance to see anyone in the car?" asked Homicide.

"No."

The porch light came on and Cap walked out of the crib. Homicide yelled, "Cap, I need to get somethin' out of the trunk. Watch my back!"

Cap grabbed two heaters and went to the car with Homicide. Homicide pulled the pump out of the trunk. Cap and Homicide walked backwards with their heaters drawn as they went back into the house.

The police took 30 minutes to arrive. As Bashi spoke to the police beside the car, everyone in the house watched from the living room window. Bashi knew deep inside that someone must have a hit out on him, which meant that he had to step up security for his protection and safety.

Homicide took the pump to his room, while Bashi and Cap entertained the skimmies. Homicide went to the tool closet to get a hacksaw and pipe file. He had never done this before, but thought it couldn't be that hard. The first thing he did was saw off the wood stock. The rest of the stock was filed nice and round. Then he put black tape around the stock and sawed off the barrel, until the rifle was 2 inches long.

"Yeah, this is short enough."

He began to file the end of the barrel, because the inside and outside had rough edges. As he was filing the inside, he came down too fast and hard causing his hand to hit the jagged edges. Homicide's hand started to bleed. "Shit!" He got up and rushed to the bathroom to clean his hand with alcohol. He wrapped it well and put on his leather gloves to finish the job. Homicide marveled at how well the rifle looked.

"Now all I need is some shells." He put the pump under his bed, rolled a joint, and turned in for the night.

The next morning, Cap took the skimmies home. When he returned, Cap said to Bashi and the Crew, "Damn, those holes are big. We just can't sit and do nothin'."

Bashi said, "I'm 'bout to change some things 'round . . ." The Crew looked receptive to what Bashi was about to say. ". . . First, I need Homicide to take the Jetta to the shop and see 'bout gettin' us a second ride."

◊◊◊◊◊

The Crew drove to Conshohocken in a new black Ford Bronco. Bashi gave the Crew assignments for the day. Business was rolling as usual until Homicide ran into Bubbles.

"Yo Homicide, let me speak to you," said Bubbles.

"Yeah, wassup."

"I told you to stop supplying my lady with dope."

"I don't even remember who your woman is."

"Come wit me and I'll show you."

They both walked up to the bar. Bubbles opened the door and pointed to a dainty woman and said, "Her, right there."

When Homicide saw who she was, he backed away a few paces out of Bubbles reach.

"Yeah, I seen her maybe once or twice," said Homicide.

"Stay the fuck away from my bitch and don't ever come in my bar again!" shouted Bubbles.

Homicide reached under his shirt for his heater and asked, "Who the fuck do you think you are talkin' to like that?"

"Just stay the fuck away from her," said Bubbles.

"As long as she wants some work, she can get it. Her money is good wit me." Homicide walked out of the bar and headed back to the park to tell Cap what happened. Out of no where, the white dude with the red Coupe Deville drove up and asked, "Hey, are you Homicide?"

"Why?"

"Because I talked with this guy about renting my car last week."

Then Homicide recognized the white dude. "Oh yeah . . . Wassup? I'm Homicide."

"I need some work. For 3 dime bags, I'll let you rent my car for the day."

Homicide remembered the mobility he once had with his Johnnies and said, "Okay, let's do that."

"You have to bring my car back at 7pm, because I need to go pick up my wife from work." He got out of the car and tossed Homicide the keys.

In turn, Homicide gave him 3 bags and started the car. His mind was made up that he wasn't given back the car. As Homicide pulled off and the tires squealed, GQ turned to Cap and said, "That punk ass bum ain't neva gonna amount to nothin'."

When Homicide pulled up at the SB crib, Bashi was also pulling up in the Bronco and asked, "Wassup Cide?"

"Nothin' just chillin' in my new ride." Homicide told Bashi how he acquired the car and that he wasn't going back out to Conshohocken. "Bashi, I need to find work at a new location."

"I got no problem wit that. You do yo thing; and you can run yo own crew. Let's go inside and chill."

Homicide and Bashi sat in the living room watching T.V., while Bashi started kicking the bobo about how he used to work the block by himself back in the day. Then Bashi asked, "So what are you gonna do next?"

"I was thinkin' of tryin' that dude, Dai Dai, out wit some work."

"Okay, what do you have left from this mornin'?"

"I got $1500."

"A'ight take that and see wassup."

Homicide got up to leave. Bashi said, "Yo Cide, don't leave yet. Let me make a call for you."

CHAPTER 16

Homicide wondered what type of call Bashi was making on his behalf. Bashi dialed the number and must have been on hold for a while. "Hello, this is Bashi. I need some I.D. and a car title with a registration card changed ova for one of my boyz." The person on the other end spoke for a while. Then Bashi continued to say, "Okay, that will be a good time."

Bashi turned to Homicide and said, "Make sure you are back by morning. Don't be late."

Homicide gave Bashi some dap and went to the auto part store, where he bought air freshener along with a front tag plate made with the letters HSB. Afterwards he drove to kick it with Tasha for a few hours and show her that he was doing exceptionally well. Then he drove to Richard Allen projects. As he got out of the car, Dai Dai was sitting on the wall and asked, "Yo Teco, whatz poppin'?"

"Let me rap with you for a minute," said Teco, a.k.a. Homicide. They headed towards the corner store and Homicide reached in his pockets, pulled out the bundle, and gave it to Dai Dai. "Yo, don't let me down, Dai Dai."

"Man, my word is my bond." They gave each other dap and Homicide left to go see Fatboy.

After two knocks, Fatboy's sister came to the door.

"Is your brutha home?"

"Yeah, he's down there."

Homicide ran down the basement stairs. Fatboy looked at him in total shock and asked, "Man, wassup with the bald head? Do you get more skimmies wit the look?"

"For sho. What did you call me? Ummm. Oh yeah, the original Don Juan."

"You must be crazy. Where did you get that ring? That thing has more diamonds than Tiffanys."

"Stop askin' so many questions and come see my new ride."

"Now that's what I'm talkin' 'bout."

Homicide and Fatboy went outside to see the car. "Damn, this chumpie is tight!" exclaimed Fatboy. Before Homicide could put the car in gear, Fatboy turned on the radio, adjusted the bass, and jammed to Power 99.

◊◊◊◊◊

The next morning, Bashi knocked on Homicide's door and said, "Get up and get dressed."

GQ overheard Bashi's request of Homicide, which reminded her that she didn't run anything any more. Bashi having Homicide as a right hand man made her furious. GQ intentionally bumped into Homicide in the hallway. "You sho you man enough to watch Bashi's back? I'm betta suited for the job than yo dumb ass," said GQ.

Homicide said, "Bitch stop trippin'." To Homicide, the position was always about the money and women. So he never got into having a power trip.

Bashi overheard the exchange and rounded the corner with a smirk on his face and said, "Cide, let's peel out."

Bashi and Homicide rode in the Bronco to see the I.D. man, who took care of all of YBM's and SB's fake I.D.s. Even though the guy never told Homicide his name, he did give Homicide some dap and said, "Have a seat ova there."

The guy took Homicide's picture, asked for the original registration card to the car, and sat down at the computer in the back room. He punched the keys with skill and speed. In less than 15 minutes, this dude came back with a driver's license and a new registration card.

"That will be $500 Mr. Holland." Holland was the name on the license and the registration card. Homicide reached into his pocket to pay the guy. When they got into the Bronco, Homicide said, "Bashi take me to get the pickup from Dai Dai."

100

They drove right down Broad Street to Richard Allen and parked two blocks away from the street action. "Damn this chumpie is boomin'," said Bashi. The runners were back and forth from car to car making sales all day. Bashi and Homicide looked at how cars kept flowing. The local guys ran both sides, front and back. All this took place on a single block, so that the Narcs could be seen before they entered into the zone. The runners had people at all corners with walkie-talkies to communicate any movement by the Narcs.

"Come on. Let's take a walk," said Homicide as he reached under the dashboard to get his .38, which he placed in the waist of his jeans.

"Is that needed?" asked Bashi.

"Now you know; betta safe than sorry."

They walked to the middle of the action to find Dai Dai. As they walked past a group of guys, one runner asked, "Yo, whatz poppin'? You lookin' for some work?"

Homicide turned to see who was talking and replied, "No. I'm lookin' for Dai Dai. You seen him?" At the mention of Dai Dai's name, the entourage moved aggressively forward. Bashi put his right hand over his left hand to display his SB ring. Homicide did the same. Once Dai Dai's boys saw the ring, they couldn't mistake the ring for being anything other than what it represented. Homicide and Bashi heard one dude whisper, "Yo, hold up. That's them cats from SB. Look at their rings." Then he said out loud, "Who you looking for?"

"Dai Dai," responded Homicide.

As the dude pulled out of his pocket a handheld radio, Homicide was ready to grab his heater. When he turned the radio up, a screeching sound pierced Homicide's ears. Then the dude pushed the button and asked, "Dai Dai, whatz poppin'?"

Dai Dai asked, "Yo, wassup?"

"Yo, these two SB boyz lookin' for you."

"Who is it?"

The dude looked at Homicide and asked, "What's yo name?"

"Teco." When Teco, a.k.a. Homicide, said his given name, all the dudes started to back away giving Homicide and Bashi space.

"Hey that's my manz. Bring him to the cut," said Dai Dai. They took Homicide and Bashi to the center of the operation, where no one was allowed unless you were from this particular part of Richard Allen. As they walked up to the door of a high rise building, Dai Dai's security said, "I need to search you."

Homicide looked at the security dude as if he were crazy and said, "Yo homeboy, I'm not goin' in there without my heat."

"Well you can't come in here unless I pat you down," replied security.

"You call Dai Dai down here now," demanded Homicide.

"I don't take orders from you."

Just as Homicide was about to step to this pussy ass security, Dai Dai came down the steps to understand what was taking so long.

"Yo Dai Dai, he won't gimme his piece," said security.

"Teco, you can't come in here wit any heat." Just the mention of Teco's name caused the security guy to also back away in fear. Dai Dai continued to say, "I tell you what Teco, stay here. I'll bring you yo lute."

They stood in the doorway while Dai Dai ran upstairs. "Yo Cide, you don't budge an inch do you?" asked Bashi.

"If I do, that's when they get you," said Homicide.

Dai Dai came back with the lute. Homicide went to peel Dai Dai off $400. However, Dai Dai said, "That was on the strength. I wanted to see how good yo shit would sell."

Bashi looked at him impressed and asked, "How did it do?"

"That's the point. It sold fast. So, when can I do business wit you?"

"I'll let Teco know. Then he'll get back wit you. How much can you handle at one time?" asked Bashi.

"As much as you can gimme." Dai Dai stood by the door and took note of how Teco, a.k.a. Homicide, and Bashi were on point at all times as they left Richard Allen. Dai Dai knew the new partnership would be lucrative.

◊◊◊◊◊

GQ brought these two white dudes to the crib to conduct new business. When Bashi walked into the crib, GQ could see the disapproval on Bashi's face and knew that this was a major fuck-up. Lately Bashi wouldn't agree to any new partnerships unless he had concurrence from Homicide. GQ, Bashi, Cap, and the twins were seated in the living room when Homicide walked into the crib.

"Yo, wassup Homicide?" GQ asked awkwardly.

Before he sat down, Homicide stared at the twins hard and placed the heater on his lap. Everyone in the room knew that Homicide wanted to make the gun visible.

"These are the twins, Curt and Bert. You might've heard of them as the Casper twins. They are major players from the Upper Darby projects. GQ brought them here to put them down," said Cap, who was trying to break the ice.

Homicide looked at his heater and put his hand around the grip. He glanced at GQ and Cap, then Bashi. As Homicide stood up with his heater, he said, "I won't have nothin' to do wit this put down." Abruptly, he walked up the stairs to his room without saying another word.

Bashi saw the frustration in the twins' eyes and said, "You will take direction directly from GQ, no one else. That's that."

Then Bashi got up to go speak with Homicide. "What was up wit yo attitude 'bout the put down? There was no need to walk away without hearing GQ out first," said Bashi.

"You know how things are suppose to go down when it comes to bringin' new faces into SB. Bashi you made the rules, not me. I only enforce the rules you set out."

"Well let's see how the twins work out. I put them under GQ's hand only."

"What the fuck you mean you put them under GQ's hand? You let her lil' ass think she is gettin' some pull 'round here, then she will be tryin' to run things. And I'm not having it," said Homicide.

Bashi smiled. "To keep her in check, we have to give her some rope. No what I mean?"

"I hear ya. But somethin' don't smell right. She walks 'round here like her shit don't stank."

"You know what I think?" asked Bashi.

"What?"

"I think the two of you have some major chemistry goin' and both of you are in denial."

"Hell naw. I don't trust her. I ain't got a problem with women runnin' things. But mark my words. GQ is a two letter name for trouble."

"Listen, the Crew has to stick together. You will have to work it out with her. Well, enough of that. Can you hook me up wit some skimmies this weekend?"

"I'm gonna see my girl Tina tomorrow. I'll ask her if she has any homegirls who are free." Then Homicide went downstairs to watch T.V. in peace, but GQ had a beef to pick with Homicide right then and there.

Before Homicide could turn on the T.V., GQ asked in a pissed tone, "Yo, why you dis my put down like that?"

"You know why. We do things by rules and codes. What you did was out of order for SB," said Homicide.

As the temperature in the room got hotter, Homicide and GQ came face to face with each other. GQ decided she had to fight Homicide to prove that she had taken down men twice his size. As her fist came forward to punch him, Homicide's reflexes kicked in immediately. He grabbed her wrist. "Listen bitch; don't ever raise your muthafuckin' hand to me again. Who the fuck you think you are?" asked Homicide.

Out of the blue, GQ swirled Homicide around with one smooth turn and pinned his arm hard behind his back. With speed, Homicide swung his arm back around pulling her close to him chest to chest and said, "I am not questionin' yo skills. You wouldn't be in SB if you weren't good at what you do. I wasn't raised to beat on women; but if you get outta place, I'm gonna check yo ass like a street thug."

There was only silence between them. For the first time he saw GQ as his equal. Being challenged by a woman in his line of work was a new experience. Homicide felt GQ's chest rising up and down. GQ's eyes softened just a little. He felt her sweet breath against his face. Then he couldn't believe what happened next. His wood started to get hard. Homicide released her and walked away very pissed off and mad as hell.

"Don't you walk away from me. What the fuck? You scared?" asked GQ.

Back in his room, his head began to hurt. So he rubbed his temples. *"Damn, her body felt soft."* His erection got harder; and he knew he had to turn his thoughts to other things. So he smoked a joint to calm down and he fell asleep.

The next morning Bashi gave Homicide a big bomb to sell, which included $500 in green bags and $500 in red bags. Homicide was glad that Bashi trusted him enough to run his own crew. So he decided to set up shop in Pen Rose Park by the airport. As he headed to his new spot, the rain poured down. He drove up Road Island Avenue by Pascale projects off of Woodland Avenue. When he crossed the intersection, he had the green light; however, a blue Chevy Impala came out of no where and hit him broadsided. BAM!

CHAPTER 17

The collision scared the shit out of Homicide. Once his car came to a complete stop, he shook his head to gain his composure. He knew that the po po would be coming soon and that he couldn't sit at the intersection waiting for them to show up. However, he was too late. Two police cars were there immediately, as if they had been watching the entire scene.

A police officer came up to Homicide and asked, "Hello sir. Are you alright?"

"Yes. Can you believe that? I had the right of way."

"Yes sir. You did. Please pull over to the side."

Then Homicide remembered that Bashi had given him a big bomb which was on the back seat of the car. He pulled the car over to the side of the street in order to think about his next move. He saw that traffic was clear, pulled off taking a sharp right, and punched the pedal to the floor hoping that he could get away. Once he reached Bartrum Village, he got out of the car to survey the damage, which wasn't as bad as he thought.

Homicide walked around to Tina's crib. The dudes in her hood were staring as if they wanted to try him. When Homicide went into Building G, he stood in the hallway looking out of the window to see what kind of moves the dudes were making, if any. Once he saw that things were cool, he knocked on Tina's door.

"Who is it?" asked a female voice from inside.

"Teco. Is Tina home?"

"Yes, hold on."

Tina came to the door wearing a pink pajama short set. She threw her arms around Homicide; and he felt every inch of her curves as they embraced. "What are you doing ova this way?" asked Tina.

106

"Well, you know me, lookin' to surprise you."

He stepped back to get a good look at Tina's fine body. Some dude came from behind Tina, looked at Homicide, and asked, "Tina B., who's this?"

Homicide put his right hand over his left hand to display his ring.

Tina replied, "Boy, this is my friend." Then she turned to Homicide and said, "This is my younger brutha Trent."

"Yo, wassup Trent? I'm Teco." Teco, a.k.a. Homicide, shook Trent's hand to insure that Trent saw the ring."

"Yo, you down with SB?" asked Trent.

"Yeah, I'm down with SB, a major player."

"Who's SB?" asked Tina.

Homicide looked at Tina and said, "Look, don't worry 'bout that."

Tina and Homicide went into the crib. She changed into more decent clothes and came back out to keep Homicide company.

"Would you like anything to drink?" asked Tina.

"Sure, can I have some milk?" asked Homicide.

With a perplexed look, Tina said, "We don't have no milk."

Homicide walked up behind her and put his lips to her ear and whispered, "What 'bout milk from you?"

"Be nice with your mannish self," said Tina, as she pushed him away with her butt.

Trent came into the house out of breath and asked, "Teco, is that yo red Coupe Deville up the street?"

"Yeah, wassup?"

"If I was you, I would move it 'round to the front of our building before it won't be there."

Homicide rose up quickly, not wanting anything to happen to his ride. So, he followed Trent outside.

"You smoke weed, Homey?" asked Homicide.

"You know it. Why you got some?" asked Trent.

"Yeah, go tell Tina we goin' to the store. Ask her do she want anything?"

Trent ran up the steps and came back downstairs just as fast. "She said can you get her a box of Boston Baked Beans candy, Lemonheads, and a pack of Tastykake Butterscotch Krimpets, plus some milk." Homicide laughed at the milk comment.

At the corner store, Homicide paid for everything. As they walked back to the car, Trent asked, "Teco, can I ask you somethin'?"

"Yeah, go ahead."

"Can you put me on wit you?"

Homicide looked at Trent as if he were crazy. He knew if Trent fucked up that there would be a major price to pay. "I don't think that's a good move for you. Have you sold dope before?"

"No, but my homies sell; and I've been 'round them."

"So, since your boyz sell, you think you can sell too?"

"Well, I don't think it would be that hard. I have a spot I can sell at 'round the corner."

Homicide wanted to prove to himself that he could operate his own shit. "Oh really? Well take me 'round there."

"Okay. Let's roll."

"Why you tryin' to bust a move so fast with yo lil' ass? Hold on. Let me take this junk food to yo sista."

"No! If we leave, she's gonna ask where we goin'. Let's jet now." Trent wanted to prove to Homicide that he was down with whatever.

"Boy, you crazy. No woman runs me. Be cool."

Homicide took the package to Tina, gave her a kiss on the cheek, and said, "Baby, I'll be right back."

When Homicide went back outside to the car, Trent asked, "What did you say to her?"

"Look Trent, when I tell you to be cool, you do just that. I got this."

They both walked around to Building F. Before they entered the building, they observed that the traffic into the building was heavy. This had to be a crack house. The SB Crew never sold crack, just crystal flake and fish scale raw. Within 10 minutes, Homicide counted 25 fiends, or what appeared to be fiends, go and come.

Trent started to jet; however, Homicide put his arm across Trent's chest and asked, "Do you know these people who this crib belongs to?"

"Yeah, wait here. I'll be right back."

Before Homicide could stop him again, Trent was gone.

In about 3 minutes, Trent came back running to the car, and said, "Teco, I'm in. The house lady said that I can bring you in as long as you take care of the house."

"How many people are in the crib?" asked Teco, a.k.a. Homicide.

"I guess 'bout 10 to 12 crackheads."

"What 'bout dope boyz?"

"One young dude from North Philly name Baby James."

"How long has he been 'round here?"

"Not long. Just come on. You're SB."

"Did you tell those people in that crib that I'm down with SB?"

"No, not yet."

Homicide knew that Trent was lying. Trent wanted to make a big impression and become a part of Homicide's crew extremely fast; however, becoming a part of Homicide's team meant building mutual trust and confidence. Rushing into deals isn't how it goes down. Timing is everything.

They walked to the crib with Trent leading the way. When Trent opened the door, Baby James' eyes opened up, as if he had seen a ghost. Baby James remembered seeing Teco, a.k.a. Homicide, almost kill the dude at the Ivy Hill Bar.

"I didn't know that this was one of yo joints," said Baby James.

"It isn't. I'm just checkin' it out. So chill," replied Homicide. Trent liked the way Homicide took control. They could tell that Baby James was afraid that SB would take all of the action.

Then Trent took Homicide to the lady who ran the crib. As it turned out, she was also a crackhead. Homicide looked her up and down wondering how a woman of her stature could let her body deteriorate, yet prance around as if she were a queen.

"What do you charge a day?" Homicide asked knowing that she would try him.

"Gimme $100 up front." She said with those crackhead eyes bulging out of her head.

"You outta yo fuckin' mind. Who you think you dealin' wit? Some rookie?" Homicide knew how much they loved that rock which controlled them; so he continued to say, "Check this out. Up front, you either take $50 in cash or $50 in work. No more. No less."

"I'll take the work. Can I get a test?" she asked.

"Yeah, just be cool. Trent will take care of you."

As Trent and Homicide left the crack house, Homicide stepped to Baby James and said, "Yo, there is enough money for both of us. You don't have the clientele to take ova this spot. So work wit me; and you will get yours too." Without waiting for a response from Baby James, Homicide left the crib.

As he walked back to the car, Homicide schooled Trent on the game. "Only give that crackhead one red bag every hour that you're there. Here is $300 in work. Trent, don't let me down. I'm gonna tell yo sista that I gotta go."

Tina was waiting for Homicide to come back. When he walked in the door, she put her arms around his neck and asked, "Baby, what took you so long?"

"Just gettin' to know yo brutha. Hey, I need to go rap with my uncle. I'll talk wit you later."

"Can I go wit you?" asked Tina.

"No, I need to take care of some business." Homicide was hoping that Tina couldn't tell that he was lying. He didn't want her to find out that he was heavy into the street life.

As he headed to his uncle's crib down 52nd to Spruce, traffic was creeping because of protesters walking the streets. The protesters wanted justice in the 1986 conflict between the MOVE group and police. The bombing, of the apartment building which the MOVE group occupied on Osage Avenue, caused a loss of lives two years ago. Homicide knew that the wounds were still fresh and that the entire city was divided between sides. He could not forget the images on the news of an entire block of West Philly burning to the ground.

The crowd seemed to be growing by the minute; and Homicide knew that he had to get the hell away from these people before he was stuck in traffic. He hit a side street, which took him to an alternate route towards his uncle's crib.

He was looking dope boy fresh. As he knocked on the door, the people across the street were checking him out.

"Who is it knockin' on my door like that?" asked Homicide's Uncle Tony, who looked like a 20 year older version of his nephew. Along with their good looks, the Jackson men had the gift of gab. They could talk their way into or out of any situation.

"It's me uncle," replied Homicide.

"Who the hell is 'me'? . . . Hey boy, wassup wit you?"

"Nothin'. Just in the hood and thought I'd stop by."

"Come on in, boy. What you been doin' wit yo'self?"

"Well uncle you know me, just gettin' my grind on."

"You got some weed?" asked Uncle Tony. *"My uncle is just as crazy as I am."*

"Yeah. I got some sniff, sniff too."

"Is it good?"

"Of course. It's the best. Do you have time to chill ova a game of chess?"

"Now Teco, you know I always got time to beat yo ass in some chess. Even tho I taught you the game, I still have a couple of moves you don't know 'bout. Have a seat at the table."

While Homicide was relaxing and getting high over in West Philly with his uncle, GQ was setting up her own plan. She was sick of playing the role of tow man. GQ wanted to run the whole SB operation. "Money, Power, and Respect" was the name of the game; and GQ wanted it all. GQ thought, *"So Homicide thinks he can check me like a street thug. I'm not just good; I'm the best in the whole damn crew. I'll show these muthafuckas whose boss."*

◊◊◊◊◊

This was the best season of the year in Philly because the weather was cool. Homicide had been taking it easy for two weeks and had seen neither Dai Dai nor Trent during this time. Everything seemed to be going fine, until Homicide received a call from Tina, who was very upset and crying.

"Tina calm down, so I can understand you," said Homicide.

"My brutha just got . . . locked up . . . for sellin' . . . dope."

"Damn, that young buck is pushin' a lot of shit for me." Tina was unaware that Homicide was the one supplying Trent with the dope; however, he knew it was his responsibility to get Trent out of jail. "Do you know what happened?" asked Homicide.

"No, he just called me," said Tina.

"What is his bond?"

"$5,000; and we don't have that kind of money."

"Look, don't worry. I'll go get him out for you right now."

"Teco, you'll do that for me?"

"Tina, it's not what you know. It's who you know." Next, Homicide made a call to Bashi and explained that he needed $5,000 pull out money.

After Homicide hung up, he went over to Tina's crib. "Yo, I need you to ride wit me to pick Trent up." As they drove to the police station, Homicide tried to comfort her with small talk. To reassure her, he put his free hand on her thigh and said, "Look, everything is gonna be a'ight. I need to know your brutha's full name."

"Trent Campbell." She replied.

When they pulled into the parking lot, Bashi and GQ were sitting in the Bronco waiting for Homicide and Tina. Homicide pulled the red Coupe Deville beside the black Bronco. After Homicide, Bashi, and GQ got out of their rides, they went to the back of the Bronco to talk.

Tina looked over to GQ and thought, *"Who in the hell is that ho?"* Then she saw Bashi giving Homicide a brown leather bag.

"Yo, I want to meet this young buck," said Bashi to Homicide.

Homicide waved his hand motioning for Tina to get out of the car. As Homicide and Tina walked into the building she asked, "Who are those people who met us here?"

"They are my partners," said Homicide.

"Are you fuckin' that ho?"

"Hell no."

"So, she is your partner at what?" asked Tina.

"If you must know, I'll tell you later."

"One more thing, does this have anything to do with Trent talkin' 'bout SB or somethin' like that?"

"You askin' too many questions right now . . . and at the wrong time."

They walked up to the counter in the main lobby. Even though there was no line, the desk clerk took about 10 minutes to acknowledge

Homicide and Tina. The clerk was a very attractive white lady with her hair pinned back; and she had on librarian glasses. Her badge read "Russo." When Ms. Russo looked up from her paperwork, she asked, "May I help you?"

"'bout time," said Homicide.

"Yes, I need to pick up my brutha," said Tina.

"What's his name?"

"Trent Campbell," replied Homicide.

"Just a minute." Ms. Russo fingered through some 3x5 index cards and pulled one out. Then she looked over her glasses at Homicide as if he were insane. She pushed away from her desk and said, "I'll be right back." Homicide and Tina watched her go to an office, which read "Narcotics Squad" on the door. She talked with a tall black man for a few minutes and came back.

"His bond is $5,000 cash only. Sorry." She said to Homicide and Tina. Ms. Russo smiled at them as if Trent wouldn't be getting out of jail tonight. She returned to shuffling the papers on her desk.

Homicide moved closer to the counter and leaned forward in a sexy manner so that only Ms. Russo could hear him. He could tell that Ms. Russo was intrigued by his move because she started to blush.

Then Homicide asked arrogantly, "So where the fuck do we pay?"

CHAPTER 18

M s. Russo looked at Homicide appalled. The smile left her face, which became berry red. She pointed to another counter that read "Cashier." She said, "Once you have paid, bring the slip back to me."

Homicide turned to Tina and said, "Baby, take a seat. I'll be right back." He scanned across the lobby and felt as though the Narcs were taking his picture; however, he couldn't determine where the cameras were hidden. His name wasn't on file; and he didn't have to worry about Mr. Holland.

As Homicide returned the slip to Ms. Russo, she said, "When you get tired of playing with those little girls in the streets, come back and I'll show you how a real woman hits it."

Homicide asked, "Do you like it from the front or from the back?"

Before Ms. Russo could reply, Tina approached the counter to see what they were talking about. Ms. Russo said, "He'll be out shortly. Thank you."

"Yeah right," said Tina sarcastically.

When Tina turned to go back to the chair, Ms. Russo slipped Homicide a small piece of paper with her digits. Homicide placed the paper in his pocket and whispered to Ms. Russo, "My shoe size is a 13."

Just as Homicide was taking a seat, Trent came through the double doors. Trent saw Homicide and Tina immediately; and a smile came over his face.

"Wassup lil' man?" asked Homicide.

"Nothin', just glad to be outta that hell hole," replied Trent. Looking very relieved, Trent turned to Tina and asked, "Wassup sis?"

"You know that I'm gonna kill yo ass when we get home."

"Wait, I was at the wrong place at the wrong time." When Trent said this, he looked at Homicide for approval. Homicide winked at Trent confirming that things were alright.

As the three of them went outside, Homicide said, "Trent, I want you to meet someone . . . . Tina baby, go sit in the car."

Trent followed Homicide to the Bronco, where Bashi was sitting on the hood. Homicide said to Bashi, "This is Trent, my right hand runner."

"Yo, wassup Trent?" asked Bashi, who extended his hand to Trent.

"Nothin'. Gotta deal with my sista trippin' all night. That's punishment enough."

"Yep, I hear ya. I just wanted to meet you to see who is on our team."

"He handled it like a pro," said Homicide proudly. Then they gave each other dap, got into their separate vehicles, and drove off in different directions.

"Baby, where do you want to go eat?" Homicide asked Tina with a smile.

"The Gallery's Chinese joint," replied Tina.

After they arrived at the Chinese restaurant, Tina went into the ladies restroom.

"Trent what's the deal? What really went down?" asked Homicide as they followed the waitress to a booth.

"The Narcs busted the place and got all of my stuff."

"Did Baby James get locked up wit you?"

"Yeah, he was in jail wit me."

"Well, you know that's it for you."

"Why? I didn't do nothin' wrong. I need to make my money, just like you. Don't do this to me Teco. Gimme one more shot."

Teco, a.k.a. Homicide, was quiet for a moment and replied, "Okay; but this time I'll run it at night to see what's really happenin' on the streets. Shhh, Shhh, here comes Tina."

As Trent moved over and Tina sat down across from Homicide, she thought, *"I want some of Teco's good dick tonight. I wonder why he won't make any advances at me? He betta not be fuckin that ho, who was in that Bronco. She ain't got nothin' on this pussy."*

"Tina, Tina, Tina," said Homicide.

"Yes, just in deep thought." She said.

Tina took off her right shoe and slipped her toes up Homicide's leg. Homicide winked at her; and she reached over and gave him a lustful kiss. Trent was repulsed by their sexual advances and said, "You guys need to take this lovey dovey shit back to the crib."

Homicide laughed and asked Tina, "Wow, what was that kiss for?"

"Just for all you've done for my brutha and me tonight."

After they finished their meal, Homicide paid the bill and left a $20 tip. They got into the car and went straight to the Village. Before Tina got out of the car, Homicide said to her, "Trent and I need to make a run. Baby, I'll see you sometime tomorrow."

"You look tired," said Tina.

"I am; but I'll be a'ight. Trust me." Homicide gave her a soft kiss and drove off. *"I want to break her off, but not until I can take it slow. I want to make love to that thick ass."*

As Homicide pulled the red Coupe Deville around the corner of the Village, he decided to park by the sidewalk where he could watch the car from inside the crib. He reached under the dash to get his stash and the heater. Homicide pulled out 20 green bags and put the rest of the stash under the floor mat. Though there was a girl watching him, he didn't see her because he was too busy putting his heater in the waist of his jeans.

At the crack house, he gave Trent the bags. As Trent continued to sell, Homicide drifted off to sleep on the couch in the front room. When he woke up, Homicide asked, "Trent, what time is it?"

"11:30pm."

"Damn, I need to go. Come to the car wit me."

They walked out to the car together. As soon as Homicide reached the driver's side, he saw the glass on the ground from the back window. "What the fuck is this?" asked Homicide, who was now mad as hell. He pulled the door open and immediately checked under the floor mat where the stash was hidden. Then Homicide looked at Trent with the look of a killer.

"Yo man, I didn't have nothin' to do wit it. I'm on yo crew. Remember?"

Homicide heard someone making a noise, "Psst! Psst! Psst!" He turned around; and this nice looking skimmie, with perfectly plump cleavage, was hanging outside of an apartment window. She waved Homicide over to her. As he looked up in her direction, she said, "I seen who broke in yo car." She was chewing and popping bubbles with her chewing gum.

"Who did it?" asked Homicide.

"Those girls whose crib you ova."

"Are you sure 'bout that?"

"Yeah, I sat right here and watched them."

"How I know you didn't do it?" asked Homicide.

"You don't. Let me put it this way. I hate them crackhead hoes. That bitch Trisha stole my man. And I hope you put her black ass to sleep. I'm the dime not her."

"What's yo name?" asked Homicide.

"Joy."

"Well Joy, you need to let him go. He's obviously outta his damn mind to leave a dimepiece like you."

Joy raised her eyebrow and smiled as she watched Homicide walk back to the car.

Homicide looked at Trent and said, "Gimme the money; and go straight home. Don't come back here. I mean it." Homicide then started the red Coupe Deville's engine and left the door open. As he walked softly up the steps of Building F, he pulled out his heater, pointed it in the window, and let off six rounds. "Pow! Pow! Pow! Pow! Pow! Pow!" Not caring if he had hit anyone, he arrogantly walked to his car.

The next voice he heard said, "Someone call the po po!"

Homicide got into the car and drove away pissed off. This was definitely not a good day or even a good night for HSB. *Damn, if it ain't one thing, it's another.*

As he reached the SB crib, Homicide started to tell Bashi what just went down. However, Bashi was already watching it on the local news. Then Homicide noticed something strange. GQ and Bashi were in the crib alone. After the first attempted hit on Bashi's life, Bashi had changed the hours of operation around to nights in order for SB to lay low and to dodge the Narcs. There was no way in the world that Cap was suppose to be out on the block by himself without backup. Homicide had a concerned look on his face. Then there was a knock on the door. Lisa and Sonya came into the living room to chill with Bashi; so, Homicide went upstairs to his bedroom in order to go to sleep and rest his nerves.

Around 3am, someone was banging on Homicide's bedroom door. Boom! Boom! Boom! "Homicide! Homicide! You need to get up right now. It's an emergency. Homicide wake up!"

He immediately grabbed his pump from under the bed and asked, "Who the fuck is bangin' on my door like their outta their fuckin' minds?"

"Boy stop trippin'. It's GQ, we need you downstairs. Now!"

When Homicide and GQ got downstairs, Cap was sitting on the couch. There was blood all over his face; and the knot on his temple was protruding from the right side of his head. Caps mouth was twisted; and there was a tooth missing.

"What the fuck happened to you?" asked Homicide.

"I can't remember. All I know is when I was gettin' ready to sell some dope to this white dude, someone hit me ova the head wit somethin'. They kept poundin' me. Then they drug me to the alley and robbed me." Homicide could tell Cap was in pain as he spoke.

"You know what time it is." Bashi said to Homicide.

"Yeah, I do boss."

Then Homicide overheard GQ talking on the phone. "Hey Curt, you both need to get ready. Yep. Yep. Did you call him? Yep. It's on."

"Ready for what? The twins ain't wit SB to be gettin' ready for nothin'." No one in SB really knew the full ramifications of what GQ was scheming to do; however, hearing her on the phone with Curt made it clear that she was up to no good.

Homicide began to load the pump with a gangster's mixture of shells, pellets, and punkin balls. He reloaded his heater with six lead split tips, which would do just the right amount of damage. Then he put on his black three quarter length trench coat, black gloves, and his shoulder holster. He looked at his Rolex watch, which stated 4am. This was a perfect time for him to head to Conshohocken.

When he arrived on the block, he turned his car lights off and rode slowly down the street. He didn't see any movement; so he parked the car on a side street next to the bar. When he entered the bar, he started to look at people's hands.

"What I tell you? You ain't wanted here," said Bubbles.

Homicide showed Bubbles the pump under his coat and said, "I'm not tryin' to cause you any trouble. I'm lookin' for someone." Bubbles froze in his tracks. Homicide walked into the pool room; however, it was empty. Raising his hand in the air, Homicide signaled to Bubbles that he was leaving.

At the crack house where Bashi set up a post for the fiends, Homicide kicked the door open. Boom! He was surprised that there were only three people in the house. He proceeded to punch the closest person to him. As Homicide continued to beat the dude by using the butt of the pump, Homicide yelled, "Who the fuck did that to Cap?!"

The second man said, "We don't know. Please don't hit him any more. We didn't do it."

"Well who the fuck did it?"

CHAPTER 19

Homicide pointed the pump at them. With his left hand, he gripped the handle and trigger; and with his right hand, he gripped the wood sled. With firmness, he pulled the sled back towards his body cocking the pump one time. The pump made a loud noise. Chuck! Chuck! As the shell jumped into the upper chamber of his toy, Homicide started to pull the trigger. A noise by the back door startled him; and he heard footsteps up the alley. Homicide ran out the back door, down the steps, and into the alley where he saw someone getting away. So, he went back into the crib to further interrogate the men whom he left in the house. However, the crib was now empty. He was ticked off and wasn't making any progress; so he decided to go back to the SB crib.

He knew that this battle was far from over. Someone had to lie down for stealing from SB. As he walked into the living room, everyone was waiting to hear the news. Homicide explained to them that he found no one. This meant that the SB Crew had to be ready to take this to the streets. Homicide knew he had to get as much rest as possible, because the Crew had to handle their business later in the day.

Homicide woke up earlier than he expected. He oiled his pump to make sure his toy was ready for war. He put on his black sweat pants and black hoodie to have a more thuggish look. Then he shaved his head to have a clean appearance for today's action. After he took out his Pay Me Stick and placed it on the bed, Homicide popped in a tape and played "Rebel Without a Pause" by Public Enemy. The song put him in the right frame of mind for the task at hand. Homicide was ready to engage in an armed revolt against whoever got into his way.

When he reached the bottom of the stairs with his Pay Me Stick and the pump in his hand, he overhead GQ on the phone again; and she was speaking to someone in a very suspicious tone. *"What the fuck is she up to?"* He sat on the sofa to put on his black Top Ten Adidas, black leather gloves, and his shoulder holster.

He decided not to confront GQ; so he headed outside to get into the red Coupe Deville. He pulled the pump from under his coat to put it on the back seat, where he covered the pump with a white towel for easy access. Then he put the Pay Me Stick on the floor and started the engine. Bashi and GQ came out of the house. GQ got into the Jetta behind the driver's seat, while Bashi sat on the passenger's side. When they pulled out of the driveway, the Jetta was the lead car.

They drove to Conshohocken; however, there was not a soul in sight. Then they drove the back roads to Norristown, which was the next town over. When they turned on Main Street, GQ rolled down her window and said, "Yo Trey, come ova here!" Then GQ pulled the Jetta over to the side of the street. Homicide pulled up close, directly behind the Jetta. GQ got out of the car and started arguing with Trey about some money that Trey owed Bashi.

Then a black Bronco pulled right behind Homicide boxing in his red Coupe Deville. *"What the hell is this?"* Because the Bronco's glass was tinted, Homicide couldn't make out who was in the SUV for sure. *"That betta be Cap."*

GQ wasn't really handling the Trey situation fast enough for Homicide. As Homicide got out of the car, Bashi yelled out of the Jetta window, "Yo Homicide, take care of this!" Homicide went back to the red Coupe Deville and pulled out the Pay Me Stick. Bashi continued to say, "Homicide beat him down and put him to sleep!"

Homicide first hit Trey on the back of the legs to drop him. Then Homicide hit Trey on his knees and his back, which caused enough pain for Trey to roll over. With severe force Homicide hit Trey right in the nuts with the bat. Only the sound of the bat swinging and Trey screaming could be heard in the streets. At first, Homicide didn't even notice that a crowd was gathering around him. Since having witnesses is never in the plan, Homicide ran back to the red Coupe Deville to jet.

He realized that the Jetta's engine was off and that GQ, who had the keys to the Jetta, was no where to be found. *"Where in the fuck did that bitch go?"* Then Homicide screamed back at the Bronco, "Move! Back up!" The driver of the Bronco put the car in reverse, back into drive, and hit the gas. All Homicide could hear were tires squealing.

Unfortunately, the call out to the Bronco driver was too late. When he looked into the rearview mirror, Homicide saw a big black 4x4 truck pulling up behind him. With his hand on the gear shift, Homicide turned the ignition and put the red Coupe Deville into drive to tap the Jetta out of the way. Glancing into his side view mirror, all Homicide saw were red and blue flashing lights pulling up beside him.

Then out of the blue, GQ hopped back into the Jetta, started the engine, and took off. To his left, he saw an officer getting out of the police car. Just as he started to gun it to the floor, a third police car pulled at an angle in front of him.

In his mind he heard Mr. G's voice loud and clear. *"Always do what you always did; and you will always get what you always got."*

"Damn!" exclaimed Homicide. As he turned his head back to the left, all Homicide saw in the corner of his left eye was the barrel of the police gun. The police officer said, "Don't move muthafucka! Turn the car off; put your hands on the dash so I can see them." Homicide did as he said.

The officer grabbed Homicide out of the car, slammed him on the hood, and asked, "Who was that in the blue Jetta?"

"I don't know what you're talkin' 'bout," replied Homicide.

"Tell me was that Mujaheed Bashi Fiten in that car? Was the driver a male or female?" asked the Officer, who knew how Bashi looked from previous investigative work.

"The driver was a male," replied Homicide.

The cop smacked Homicide on the back of his bald head and said, "Tell me what the fuck you doin' in Norristown."

"Fuck you pussy," said Homicide.

The officer put handcuffs on Homicide, read him his Miranda rights, shoved him into the police car, and drove away to the local police station. While traveling in the car, Homicide could hear the call over the police car radio. "There's no sign or sight of a blue Jetta with a male driver. Over."

When they put Homicide in the tank, he could only think about the toys in the back seat of the red Coupe Deville. *"Shit! What the fuck just happened?" This isn't suppose to go down like this. How did the police show up so fast on Main Street? Were they waiting for me?"*

Homicide heard keys rattling, which opened the tank door. "Hey you bald head, come on," said the officer, who then grabbed Homicide by the arm and led him to an interrogation room with no windows. "Have a seat right there."

The officer who arrested him on Main Street came into the room and said, "We just want to ask you some questions." Then he pulled out a tape recorder and pushed the record button. "I'm Officer Jones #5973."

"I'm Officer Beasley #1356," said the officer who brought him into the room.

"Officer Beasley and I would like to ask you some questions about today's scene. Is that alright with you?"

Homicide looked at both of them and said, "I don't have nothin' to say to you two dicks."

Officer Jones thought he might try Homicide any way and asked, "Do you know Mujaheed Bashi Fiten and Gail Indigo Que, a.k.a. GQ?"

Homicide looked at both of them and shook his head from side to side to symbolize an answer of no.

"We need you to answer into the recorder," said Officer Beasley.

Homicide shook his head again. Officer Jones got up and walked out the door. Homicide just sat there not saying a word. Then Officer Jones returned and said, "Maybe this will help you talk." He set the pump on the table in front of Homicide.

"You think puttin' that pump in my face suppose to make me talk? I don't know nothin' 'bout what happened or this pump," said Homicide.

"Well that seems real funny. We got it out of the back seat of the car you were driving," said Officer Jones.

"I don't know what you talkin' 'bout. My prints are not on that gun."

"We will see won't we?" asked Office Beasley.

"You know that pump is under legal limits. That means Fed time. Yeah, yo ass is going to jail. Take him away," said Officer Jones.

CHAPTER 20

Homicide was taken back to the tank, until it was time to go to the Norristown jail. They put Homicide in a van with 7 other people, who were being transported. Homicide observed, *"This building looks like a big ass library."* The driver came to the back to let out the inmates, who were also known as 10-95s. Homicide went through booking. He was charged with unauthorized use of a motor vehicle and possession of a dangerous weapon with no bond set at this time.

All Homicide wanted to do was to make a phone call to find out what would take place next. They moved all new inmates to an intake dorm where everyone wore green tops and bottoms. Homicide was given the opportunity to call the SB crib.

The Voice Response Unit (VRU) on the telephone started to prompt Homicide. "Please state your name."

"Homicide."

Music played for a few minutes; then the VRU stated, "Your number can not be completed as dialed. This number does not accept collect calls."

"Shit! Shit!" exclaimed Homicide.

He didn't know what the fuck to do now. So he went to lie down on the bunk in a cell. *"I sure could use a joint."* Homicide fell asleep for about 2 hours, until the loud voice of the jailer woke him up. "Count time! Count time!"

His cell-mate came over to him to exchange a little small talk. Homicide really didn't want to talk, because he was contemplating about how he could contact Bashi. *"This jail shit ain't happenin'."*

"Yo man, do you have three-way?" asked Homicide.

124

"Yeah. Why? You need to make a call?" asked the cell-mate.

"You know it; just plug me in," said Homicide.

The cell-mate called his girlfriend, Tammy Lawrence, and explained the situation. Then he handed Homicide the phone.

"Hello," said Homicide.

"What's the number?" asked Tammy.

"476-4762," replied Homicide.

"Okay, hold on for a minute." When Tammy clicked back over, Homicide heard the phone ringing.

"Hello," said Bashi.

"Yo, wassup? I'm in Norristown jail."

"Gimme a few days; then I'll get you out," said Bashi.

"I don't have a bond yet," said Homicide.

"You should be goin' to court in three days to get a bond. When you do, call me back with the amount."

"Yo, don't leave me in here." Homicide couldn't believe what he heard next. The dial tone was very clear. Then he heard a click.

"Hello. Anyone there?" asked Homicide.

"Yeah, I'm here."

"Who am I speaking wit?"

"This is Tammy."

"Thank you for the call. I'm Homicide. Look, I don't know the guy that gave me this three-way. Can I call you later for a future three-way?"

"Yes, Just tell Lamont I said to give you the number. Believe me; people helped me out when Lamont was first locked up. I've learned that fam and friends help each other out. It's a common courtesy."

Homicide turned to Lamont and said, "Tammy told me to tell you to gimme her number."

"Let me talk wit her first," said Lamont. Homicide gave him the phone; and 15 minutes later, Lamont gave Homicide a piece of paper with Tammy's digits on it.

Later that night, the jailers moved Homicide to population. As they were moving about the jail, the prisoners went to several cell blocks. The first block was Alpha. The jailer called out some names. Then they moved on to the next block, which was Beta block. To get

125

to this block, the prisoners had to go up some stairs. The jailer called out, "Johnson! Taylor! Holland . . . Holland . . . Holland!" Homicide stood there for a minute until it dawned on him that Holland was the fake name that he had on his driver's license. The jailer continued to say, "You all go in this cell block."

Homicide went to cell 154 in the corner. He stood by the bars to check out the scene. There was a T.V. playing the show "Alf." A phone and tables were also in the room. He turned to his new white cell-mate and said, "Yo, wassup? I'm Homicide."

"I'm Jerry. You're the one that was on the news this morning."

Homicide looked at Jerry in disbelief. "Yeah, I guess so." Homicide sat on his bunk. *"I want to call Rhonda; but I don't have her new number. Tina don't have no money. Me-Me probably got a block on her phone. I just gotta chill and wait."*

◊◊◊◊◊

At 7:30am on the third day, the jailer in the bubble called out, "Holland get ready for court! Holland get ready for court!"

After he got dressed, his cell door opened up. He went downstairs to the holding tank, where the other inmates were waiting to go to court. The courthouse judge read Homicide the charges and set his bond at $8,000. Homicide knew that he would be released just as soon as he could contact Bashi. When he reached the cell block, he immediately called Tammy.

When Tammy picked up the phone, the VRU stated, "You have a collect call from 'Homicide' an inmate at the Norristown County Jail. To accept the charges press or say 2 and hold. To deny the charges press 5. To block calls from this facility press 8. To end this call, hang up."

"2," said Tammy.

"Your call is being connected," stated the VRU.

"Hello," said Tammy.

"Wassup? I just got back from court; and I need to talk with Bashi."

"Okay, let me call him for you." Within a few seconds, she flashed back over and said, "Homicide, the phone is just ringing."

"Okay, hang up. Can you do me a favor please?"

"Sure, what is it?"

"Call him back in another hour and let him know that my bond is $8,000."

"Before I forget to ask you, where do you live?" asked Tammy.

"Why you askin'?" asked Homicide.

"Because this number is the same three digits as my job."

"Mt. Airy."

"My job is in Mt. Airy. Hold on let me click ova and try him once more for you." The phone rang five times before someone picked up.

"Hello."

"Yo Bashi, I went to court; and my bond is $8,000. So wassup?"

"Homicide just chill. I will have you out in two weeks, Strickly Business," said Bashi.

"Why you waiting so long to spring me Bashi?"

"Your bond may go down or you might get out on O.R."

"What's O.R.?"

"They will let you out on yo own recognizant, which means they trustin' yo ass to show back in court when they set a date," said Bashi.

"A'right, I'll give you a call later . . . . Tammy, please stay in contact with Bashi for me."

"Okay, call me in a week."

◊◊◊◊◊

Back at the SB crib, GQ was in her room relaxing. This was the moment in which she had been waiting. Cap had left the SB Crew because of the beat down. Homicide was in jail. Therefore, GQ could run things again. Then she heard Bashi's voice. "GQ, come upstairs! We need to talk."

She walked slowly upstairs into Bashi's room and asked, "Yo, wassup?"

"We need to get Homicide out in two weeks. He's the right hand; and we need him out."

"You and me started this shit. I was your first runner on the block. When no one believed in you, it was me tellin' you that you could do this. You and me closer than real fam, not Homicide or Cap. It's me. And I gave up my dream to be a model and fashion designer to watch Homicide bump me off? Oh hell no—"

"Gail, you have it all wrong. There is a hit out on my life. If I go, there has to be someone next in line to protect you. That's why, baby girl—"

"I don't need that cigarette beggin', car stealin', dick slingin' bum to protect me."

Bashi could see the hostility in GQ's hazel eyes. She didn't comprehend that Bashi loved her like family and wanted to protect her. He wasn't expecting this type of rage. Then Bashi couldn't believe what she did next. GQ pulled out a five dollar bill and some coke right in front of him. GQ took four big snorts up her nose. Bashi's eyes opened wide in disbelief.

"What the fuck are you doin'?" asked Bashi.

"What do you think? asked GQ.

"I know you are not gonna disrespect me by snortin' dope right in my face. You are actin' like you have lost yo damn mind. Sho me that you can handle this shit and run things."

"You know I can run this whole damn operation. As a matter of fact, I want half of all profits startin' today," demanded GQ.

"You buggin'. I can't trust you to obey the rules of SB. How can I trust you wit my loot?"

Bashi was pissed at the fact that GQ would approach him for half of the profits which he funded. Bashi rose up off of the bed and smacked the dope out of GQ's hand. GQ stood up and met Bashi face to face. As they both stared into each other's eyes, a loud knock on the front door broke the tension. GQ cleaned her nose and went to see who was at the door. She was hoping it was her boy, Travis.

"Who is it?" asked Bashi.

"It's for me," replied GQ.

◊◊◊◊◊

The phone rang three times and awoke Tammy from a peaceful sleep. With her eyes closed, she reached for the phone and almost knocked the phone off of the night stand.

"Hello," said Tammy.

"You have a collect call from 'Homicide' an inmate at the Norristown County Jail. To accept the charges press or say 2—"

"2," said Tammy.

"Your call is being connected."

"Hey Homicide, I've been waiting for you to call. I think somethin's wrong."

"Why you say that?" asked Homicide.

"I was suppose to hold Bashi's car for him, because he had to go out of town for some business. All of a sudden the phone to the house has been cut off, plus his pager."

"When was the last time you heard from Bashi?"

"When you asked me to stay in contact with him for you, I did. Shortly after that, he and I started kickin' it. We real tight. My job is two blocks from his house; so we have lunch every day."

"So have you talked to GQ or Cap?"

"No, Cap left the crew after you got knocked; and GQ moved in with some dude."

There was complete silence for a few seconds. Homicide spoke first. "Tammy, I don't know what to tell you. Have you been past the crib at night?"

"No, why?"

"Can you stay late at work today, drive past the crib, and tell me if Bashi's bathroom light is on or off? Will you do that for me?"

"Yes, I'll call you and see if the Jetta is there also."

They hung up and Homicide went back to the cell. While he was lying on his bunk thinking, Homicide heard a female voice from the loud speaker announce, "Holland report to the bubble. Holland report to the bubble."

"What in the hell could this be 'bout?"

The jailer came to the window and said, "You need to report to the counselor's office to sign your release papers."

Homicide didn't know what was happening. Once he reached the counselor's office, he rapped on the door twice and a woman said, "Come in." He opened the door and there stood this fine ass yellow-skinned skimmie in a two-piece suit.

"You may have a seat. My name is Ms. Beverly Jenkins." She looked at Homicide from head to toe and continued to say, "I'm going to get right to the point. The courts want to release you on O.R., but I think your ass should stay in jail." Homicide looked at her and smiled. She then asked, "Do you know what O.R. means Mr. Holland?"

Homicide replied, "O.R. means that the judge is allowing me to go free without posting bail solely on my promise to appear back in court." Homicide believed in always being prepared. Shortly after Bashi broke it down to him what O.R. meant, Homicide went to the Legal Library and found the definition.

"Very impressive Mr. Holland. You are much more astute than I thought you were."

"Don't let my good looks fool you, Ms. Jenkins." Homicide said with a smirk.

"I see. You are free to go Mr. Holland. Make sure you show back up in court."

Homicide got up to leave; and he was elated that he was going home to the SB Crew. When he reached the cell block, he went to call Tammy; however, she didn't answer the phone. Time seemed to stand still. The jailer still hadn't called his name. When 9:00pm hit, Homicide called Tammy one more time, hoping that she would be home.

"Hello," said Tammy.

"You have a collect call from 'Homicide' an inmate at the Norristown County Jail. To accept the charges press or say 2—"

"2," said Tammy.

"Your call is being connected."

"I know I was to call you at 9:30pm; but I've just been release on O.R.," said Homicide.

"Homicide stop playin'," said Tammy.

"I'm serious Tammy. All I'm waiting on is for them to call my name. So what did you see?"

"I seen his Jetta; but the lights to his bathroom was out. What does that mean?"

CHAPTER 21

Homicide's mind was racing; and he knew that he would face problems once he was released from jail. "I'm sorry Tammy. What did you say?"

"What does the lights being out mean?"

"It's a code. If the lights are on, everything is okay. If the lights are ever out, then somethin's wrong in the crib. That light is to never be turned off by Bashi. Only his fam and me knew this. No one else in the SB Crew knew."

"So you think somethin' has happened to Bashi?"

"I don't know; but I'll find out tonight."

Tammy told Homicide where she worked, so that he could come to see her when he got out. Before he could hang up the phone, the jailer shouted, "Holland A-T-W! Holland A-T-W! All The Way Out!"

"That's me Tammy. I'll see you tomorrow. Peace Out," said Homicide.

Homicide went through booking. He was glad that he was going and not coming this time. They gave him all of his personal property in a paper bag. He signed his name one last time before he was released. "You can go through that door," said the intake officer, who pointed to a grey door. Once Homicide reached the door, he heard a loud click and pushed the door open. The next place Homicide stopped was at the cashier counter, where he was given his money. Then he waited for a little shuttle bus to take him to SEPTA. After one bus transfer, Homicide was on the corner of Williams Avenue. From there he had to walk four blocks to reach the SB Crib. He became nervous the closer he got to the crib. His adrenaline started to pump him up. He was ready for war, if necessary. He could feel his heart beating faster than normal. *"I need to calm down before I reach the crib."*

As Homicide approached the crib, the notion dawned on him that he had left his keys to the house on the key ring of the Coupe Deville, which had been impounded. He thought of how happy Bashi would be to see him. Just as he started going up the steps, he noticed that all of the lights were off and that the Bronco and Jetta were also gone. Since no one was at the SB Crib, Homicide didn't want to leave his paper bag with his belongings at the front door. After jumping the fence, he was expecting the dog to come out of the dog house. *"What the hell happened to the dog?"*

Homicide knew that he had to find Bashi. So he went around to Fatboy's crib to chill out and make a few calls.

"Yo homey, wassup?" asked Homicide.

"Man, I thought you were on lock down," said Fatboy.

"I was. I just got out 'bout 2 hours ago. Have you seen the crew?"

"Naw, not really . . . . Just off and on . . . ."

"Well look, I need to make a few calls."

"The phone is ova there."

"Where's the weed, Fathead?" asked Homicide.

Homicide walked to the phone. He paged Bashi; however, Tammy was correct. The recording stated that the number had been disconnected. Homicide thought this to be strange. He held the receiver in his hand for a few minutes thinking about what to do next. For both GQ and Cap, Homicide left voicemail messages that stated, "This is Homicide. I just got out. Meet me at the crib in twenty."

While waiting in the basement of Fatboy's crib, Homicide and Fatboy smoked some weed and played the arcade game Centipede by Atari.

"Fatboy, I need to go check to see if anybody has come to the SB crib. I'll check you later."

Just as Homicide turned the corner, he saw that the lights were on in the SB living room. He had no heat on him, which was a major disadvantage. He noticed that the Jetta was in the driveway. Just before he reached the crib, a Bronco pulled up. He thought this to be Cap; however, both car doors swung open. Scoping out the scene, Homicide stopped in his tracks and posted up behind a tree. The more he looked at the Bronco, he realized that this was the same Bronco that boxed him in the day he was arrested at Norristown. As he looked closer, this Bronco wasn't the one that belonged to Bashi. There was a curly black haired dude stepping out from the driver's seat. *"What the fuck is he doin' here?"* Then from the passenger's side appeared Cap. *"This shit don't look right. Where is Bashi?"*

Homicide continued to walk to the crib and rapped on the door. Knock! Knock! Knock!

"Who is it?" asked GQ.

"It's Big Cide."

GQ opened the door a few inches to see if it really was Homicide. When she saw him, a smile came over her face and she breathed a sigh of relief. Because GQ always portrayed a gangster's persona, Homicide tried to remember if he had ever seen GQ smile before.

"Wassup Cide?" asked GQ.

GQ had a heater concealed behind the back waist of her jeans. When Homicide stepped into the living room, GQ gave him a big hug. That's when he felt the gun. She stepped back away from him with a troubled look on her face. As he gave Cap some dap, Homicide asked, "Who's the new guy? And wassup with the long faces?"

"This is my man, Travis D. Travis D. this is Homicide," said GQ.

Homicide turned to Travis and said, "Didn't I see you at Gerrets Lounge a—"

"Listen, somethin' has happened. Come here and let me show you what we just found," said GQ.

As GQ and Homicide walked up the stairs, Homicide started to see blood spots on the carpet leading to Bashi's bedroom. Deep inside Homicide knew that this wasn't good. Homicide and GQ went into the room and opened the door. The first thing Homicide noticed was the large piece of carpet missing. Also there were a lot of cleaning bottles all over the room.

"Damn, I can't breathe up here," said GQ, who ran back down the stairs.

Touching nothing, Homicide left out of the room and went to his bedroom to get his .38, which was in a hole in the wall of closet. To his surprise, the gun was still there. When he came downstairs, Homicide was holding the big black heater in his hand. Everybody stood up and looked to Homicide for his theory of what might have happened. GQ was becoming even more distressed.

"What do you think happened? Did Bashi kill someone? Did someone kill Bashi? How in the world did someone get into the crib? When could it have happened? Who is out to get Bashi? Maybe Bashi flipped and killed the dog. Where is the damn dog?"

"Look, just calm down and let me think," said Homicide. He looked at everybody. With the heater in his hand, Homicide motioned for everybody to sit down.

"Okay, tell me when was the last time anyone saw Bashi," said Homicide.

Everyone was focused on the .38 in Homicide's left hand, until GQ started to retrace Bashi's tracks.

"Bashi and I were at the SB Crib. Then Travis came over to get the rest of my stuff, 'cause there was no need of stayin' here. Without you and Cap, it's not the same. Bashi called me back to the crib and asked me to take him to the bus station, so he could make the trip to New York. I did. After I dropped Bashi off, I kept the Jetta and drove back to Travis' crib. The bus station was the last place I saw Bashi. I don't have a contact for him in New York. He should have been back by now. What do we do next?"

"We can't call the cops, 'cause too much shit is here," said Cap.

"So, we gotta figure this out on our own," said Travis.

"I'm thirsty," said GQ.

"Baby, let's go get somethin' to drink," said Travis.

When Travis and GQ went into the kitchen, Homicide looked at Cap and asked, "How in the hell did Travis D. get into the SB Crew?"

"GQ brought him in when Bashi went out of town. At least that's what she told me . . . ."

"Do you know where Bashi went to?"

Homicide could see that Cap was hesitant to speak or was even afraid of something. "Homicide, I don't know and that's Strictly Business."

As Homicide looked Cap in the eyes, Homicide knew that Cap was telling the truth. Homicide started to think of a plan to find out what really happened to Bashi. As Homicide sat in the living room, he could feel death all around; and it didn't sit well that Bashi was missing in action.

"Yo GQ! I need to holla at you and Travis D!" shouted Homicide.

While in the kitchen, GQ looked at Travis and asked, "What the fuck do he want now?" GQ and Travis came out of the kitchen with aggravated looks on their faces.

Homicide asked, "GQ, why did Bashi go to New York?"

"He went to New York, because he owed some people a lot of money; and when he got back, he was suppose to let GQ and me know," said Travis.

"Okay look, we need to figure out what went wrong, because somethin' must have happened when he got back from New York."

"So what are we gonna do?" asked Cap.

"We need to think of anybody that might want to do Bashi harm and create a list."

"Let's see. There was that dude at the Ivy Hill Bar that you beat up. Remember the dude who got pissed that Bashi was dancin' wit his woman?" asked Cap. Everyone nodded.

"Bubbles hated Bashi's ass," said GQ.

"I made a run with Bashi one night and took care of a problem he had in Summerville," said Homicide. GQ gave Homicide a cold look, because this confirmed that Homicide was taking care of SB business without her knowledge; and she didn't like this at all.

"What 'bout the drive-by? And the fools that tried to take me out?" asked Cap.

"What 'bout Trey? He could have wanted revenge," said Homicide.

"Lisa got really ticked with Bashi, after Bashi hooked up with Tammy. Tammy is a dime compared to Lisa and Sonya. Isn't there a sayin' 'bout a woman's scorn?" asked Cap. GQ shot Cap an evil look.

"What 'bout Dai Dai? He wanted to become a major player with SB. Maybe we weren't movin' fast enough for his pace," said Homicide.

After they agreed on the names, everybody agreed to check out someone on the list. Homicide decided that he wanted to personally talk with Bubbles and the people in the Ville.

"Look, before we split up and go see these people, here is the deal. If any of them act stupid, get back wit me. Cap, gimme yo pager. We will have to tell Bashi's fam soon and they will want to call the police. Yo GQ, I need a ride to get around in. Then we will review the list of suspects in 48 hours. That's all we got." Homicide was demonstrating definite control over the operation to find Bashi; and GQ didn't like this shit.

"Yo GQ, I need you to open the back door so that I can get my bag." said Homicide.

"What bag are you talkin' 'bout?" asked GQ, who was looking at Homicide as if he were crazy.

"The one I put at the back door when I got out," said Homicide.

"The back door is boarded up to make sure no one breaks in. So let's just go out the front and around," said GQ.

GQ and Homicide went out the front door to get Homicide's paper bag. Just as Homicide was about to climb the fence, GQ said, "Yo wait, I got a key to the lock on the fence. I'll go get the bag for you," said GQ. Though Homicide thought it was odd for GQ to have a key to the fence, he gave it no more thought.

Once GQ got the bag, she came back towards Homicide. Before GQ reached him, she quickly stepped into the garage for a minute. She left the garage door halfway open, gave Homicide the bag, and locked the fence.

"Homicide go put that stuff up and come ride wit me. I need to go make a call to Bashi's sister, Maya."

"Didn't we say we were gonna check 'round before we told Bashi's fam?" asked Homicide.

"We did. I am gonna ask her to meet wit us tomorrow. We need to tell her that Bashi is missin' before the word gets out on the streets. She needs to hear it from us. Can you go wit me?"

"Sure."

On the way to the phone booth, Homicide pressed GQ for more information about Bashi. "Yo tell me somethin'. Is it true what Travis D. said 'bout why Bashi left Philly?" asked Homicide.

"Yep, he went to New York due to him owing the Italians some money. He went to get the loti up."

Homicide thought for a moment and determined that this reason had to be untrue. Bashi made big bank; his account was fat. GQ pulled over to a pay phone on Vernon Road to make her call. Because of her hand gestures and body language, GQ had to be fussing with someone on the phone. Homicide didn't think that GQ would be talking to Maya in such fury.

After GQ returned to the Jetta, she said, "Ok, I will take you ova to Travis' crib to get Bashi's Bronco for you to drive."

"I need to put this bitch on my list," thought Homicide.

CHAPTER 22

At Travis' crib, GQ went inside to get the keys to Bashi's Bronco. Homicide started to go inside as well; but he changed his mind after he heard a vicious dog barking. *"Does everyone have a mean ass dog?"*

After Homicide got into Bashi's Bronco, he set out on his mission to check out the top suspects on the list, just to be sure that shit was covered. Trey was still in the hospital, so Homicide marked Trey off of the list. The people, who owed money to Bashi, in Summerville were dead. He wondered if they had any alliances whom he should be concerned about. Bashi had all the contacts in Summerville; and with less than 48 hours to investigate, Homicide wondered if talking to people there would be worth his time. However, he decided to make a quick swing through the area anyway. Then he thought back to the dude he beat up at the Ivy Hill Bar. *"That dude was a pussy. There is no way he would be goin' after Bashi, especially wit me as the SB enforcer."* Homicide crossed the Ivy Hill Bar dude off of the list as well.

The first place Homicide went was to Bubbles' local bar. When he walked in the bar, Bubbles looked at Homicide with a shocked look on his face and said, "When yo black ass get out of jail? I told you—"

"Yeah, yeah, you told me 'don't sell dope in yo bar. And don't mess wit yo woman.' I got it. I got it." Everyone sitting at the bar laughed. They too had heard Bubbles give this speech to Homicide several times. Homicide continued to say, "Yo Bubbles, I ain't here to disrespect you. I need to rap with you for a moment." Bubbles looked at his customers and motioned for Homicide to follow him to the other end of the bar where they could have some privacy.

"Wassup Homicide?" asked Bubbles.

THE STREET LIFE SERIES: IS IT SUICIDE OR MURDER?

"Look, you are right; I just got out. Bashi is missin'. Have you seen him or anything strange on the block?"

"Well, right after you got locked up . . . I'd say it was two weeks ago . . . . GQ and this new guy, Travis D., started working the block together. I heard GQ tell somebody in the pool room one day that she was runnin' shit now. SB belongs to her."

"Oh word? Did you hear who beat up Cap?"

"Naw, I only heard that you whoop some dude's ass that night."

"Does Cap work the block wit GQ and Travis D.?"

"I haven't seen Cap since the night of the beat down."

"You see a lot of people come in and out of the bar. You have a good judge of character. Who do you think would be a prime suspect?"

"Ummm. Who has the most to gain from Bashi's disappearance? That's who I would try to find. You know most crimes are domestic or committed by people that the victim already knows. Maybe you need to look inside before you look outside."

"I'll give that some thought. Well, how is yo wife?" asked Homicide teasingly.

"If you don't get the hell out of my bar, I'm gonna whoop yo ass myself," said Bubbles; and they both laughed.

Homicide left the bar and went to Summerville. He had to be very careful around this hood and not to ask the wrong people questions. He saw some crackheads on the street corner and decided to ask them for information. Crackheads always seemed to know the 4-1-1.

"I'm lookin' for a dude named Mujaheed Bashi Fiten. We call him Bashi. Have you heard anything?" asked Homicide.

"Man, don't mention his name 'round here. Some dude got jumped just for mentionin' Bashi's name to this female they call GQ. Bashi is the butta king. His shit is straight like that. I really miss—"

"Wait, wait, back up for a minute. What did you say 'bout this GQ person?" Homicide was surprised that this crackhead mentioned GQ.

"Oh yeah GQ, she drives a blue Jetta and now supplies dope to the Ville. She put a couple of dudes in the hospital when they owed her money. Everyone is terrified of her in the Ville."

"So was it easy for her to take ova this block?" asked Homicide.

"Hell yeah. She runs that SB Crew. She got a ring and everything. I ain't neva seen a woman in the hood move as fast as GQ. You gotta give her props. She the man . . . ." Then the crackhead laughed and continued to say, "I ain't mad at her. She hooked me up a couple of times just for keepin' watch for her."

"Does she work wit anybody?"

"Yeah, some dude that drives a black Bronco, just like yours. He act like GQ his girl, 'cause when my boy, Bobby, made a sexual advance at GQ, the Bronco dude hit Bobby in the jaw and broke it. I have no idea what the Bronco dude sees in her. She dress like a tom boy. Maybe it's her eyes—"

"Listen, 'preciate that 4-1-1. Here is a 20." Everything seemed to be pointing to GQ and Travis. *What could be the motive for them to take out Bashi? Was it the money? Bashi gave GQ all the money she needed. Was it the power? GQ wanted me out of the picture. Why didn't she take me out? Why would she kill Bashi? Bashi loved GQ like fam. This isn't addin' up.*

After Homicide finished talking to those ghost chasers from the Ville, he sat in the Bronco in a daze. *What happened to Bashi? GQ had to have somethin' to do wit this shit. That bitch is fake as hell. I need to be sure that I check out everybody. Trust no one. Everybody is a suspect.* Then Homicide's eyebrow went up. *Shit! Why didn't I think of them?*

Homicide started Bashi's Bronco. Before he pulled off, he checked his heater and placed it on the passenger's seat. He drove 10 minutes and located the house where Bashi had taken him when Homicide was first put down. There were rules to SB and Homicide was about to break Rule #6. *What the hell, at this point all the rules have been broken.* He put his heater in the waist of his pants and put his shirt over it. As he walked up the steps, Homicide was ready to fire down on anyone who tried him. He had no tolerance. Shoot first; ask later.

"Who is it?" asked Yusef.

"It's Homicide SB."

As the locks started to turn, Homicide put his left hand on his heater and turned sideways to the door, just in case some shots were fired. Yusef's face looked Homicide up and down.

"You hot?" asked Yusef?

"Yeah."

"Well let me see it."

Homicide showed Yusef the gun by pulling up his shirt. As Yusef let Homicide into the YBM Crib, Homicide could see that he came at the wrong time. Or was his timing right? All of the big bosses of YBM were sitting at the dining room table. When they saw Homicide, they stood up.

"Homicide please come and have a seat," said Rasheed.

"Can you put yo gun on the table?" asked Basil.

Contemplating whether he should put his heater on the table, Homicide knew that things would go to another level if he ignored the request. As he laid the heater on the table, Homicide was trying to anticipate their next move.

Lil' Tim said, "Homicide you have come to us at a very awkward time. Nevertheless, we might be able to use yo help."

"If it's dealin' with findin' Bashi, then yes, I've come at the right time," said Homicide.

"Sit and join our meetin'. What you hear today will never be repeated to anyone. Is that understood?" asked Lil' Tim.

"Yeah, I dig," said Homicide.

"Okay. Bashi told me that he was goin' to New York. We have called every train station, bus station, and airport. There's no sign of Bashi comin' or goin'. Yusef has put a team on watch at the house in case Bashi did show up," said Basil.

"Homicide when you showed up that threw us for a spin. We knew that you had been taken down and wasn't to get out until Bashi bailed you out. We thought shit was alright," said Yusef.

"Look, all we need to know is do you have anything to share wit us 'bout where Bashi is?" asked Rasheed.

"No, I don't have shit to tell you. I'm here to see if one of y'all have somethin' to tell me. At this point, everyone is a suspect in YBM," said Homicide.

Basil's eyes widen in disbelief about Homicide's statement. Basil said, "Wait homey, just calm down. Bashi's my brutha, my blood brutha. So I can understand why you upset; however, this fight is ours, not yours. We'll handle things from here."

"Wait, wait homey. I don't know if you realize what Bashi has done for me since I've been put down. This is OUR fight," said Homicide who grabbed his heater off of the table and stood up. They saw the sincerity in Homicide's face. At that moment, Homicide was off the hook as a suspect with the YBM Crew.

As Homicide put the heater under his shirt, he said, "With all due respect. I hope you find them or whomever before I do." He opened the door and left the YBM crib. *I need to find out what happened before Bashi's bruthas do. I owe Bashi that.*

His next stop was Richard Allen projects. As he drove, all types of shit were running through his mind; and he had to figure out how to get everything back under control. However, he needed more fire power. If Dai Dai wasn't a threat, he would be the one to go to for whatever Homicide needed. Just as Homicide pulled up to the corner store, Homicide could see Dai Dai chilling with his homies. As Homicide got out of the Bronco, Homicide put the .38 in his hip. Dai Dai noticed Homicide coming; however, Dai Dai never became nervous, which was a sign Homicide had been looking for in all suspects.

"Whatz poppin' Teco? Yo gurl GQ just came by earlier."

"Oh really? What did she want?"

"She was talkin' 'bout Bashi being missin'. She had the nerve to ask me if I kidnapped him. I told her that she must be outta her damn mind."

"Look can we walk and talk?" asked Homicide.

"Sure, gimme a few minutes," requested Dai Dai.

Dai Dai gave a bag of dope to one of his runners and walked with Homicide. Homicide asked, "When was the last time you seen Bashi?"

"It was the last time I seen you two together."

"Did you get upset with Bashi when he didn't get back wit you on sellin' for SB?"

"Naw, I got a lot of work. I just liked Bashi's shit. It sells fast. I ain't gonna kill nobody for no damn reason. I got no beef with Bashi."

"Do you also know Travis D. from Norristown?"

"No . . . . Wait, I did hear somethin' 'bout some new players on the blocks in South West Philly. GQ also said somethin' 'bout she was gonna check out some dude name Trent from Bartrum Village to see if he had somethin' to do wit Bashi's disappearance."

"What? Trent is in my Crew. There is no way in hell Trent would be involved in this. Hey, I need some big heat for a job," said Homicide.

"You know I got you. Come wit me," said Dai Dai.

He took Homicide to this apartment not to far from the store. Dai Dai knocked on the door with a certain rhythmic beat. Then the door came open. Dai Dai walked towards some guy and whispered in his ear. The security dude kept his focus on Homicide.

"Teco go wit him and he'll take care of you," said Dai Dai.

After Homicide got a Beretta .45, he went back to the crib. As he pulled beside the curb to park, the Jetta and Travis' Bronco were already there. When Homicide got out, he put the Beretta under the front fender of Bashi's Bronco in case he needed it later. He felt that the next couple of hours were do or die. Once he entered the house, he went straight to his bedroom without saying a word to anyone in the crib. While he was chilling in his room trying to piece together the mystery of Bashi's disappearance, there was a knock on the front door. Travis opened the door; and there stood Lisa, who came to the crib looking for Bashi.

"Lisa, what do you want?" asked GQ.

"I want to know where is Bashi?" asked Lisa.

At the mention of Bashi's name, Homicide came downstairs to see what was going on. Lisa was looking at Travis in a very seductive manner.

"Bitch, what the fuck you lookin' at him like that for?" asked GQ.

"He's fine. Who's that?" asked Lisa.

"Bitch, that's my man," said GQ, who punched Lisa on the jaw. Lisa returned with a counter blow, which hit GQ on the nose. GQ followed up with three more blows to Lisa's mouth. Travis grabbed GQ, in order to spare Lisa any more pain.

"What the fuck you doin'?" asked Homicide.

"That bitch ain't nothin' but a ho," said GQ.

Blood was all over the carpet as Lisa bled from her lip.

"Calm down. Calm down," said Homicide.

"Lisa, you need to get the fuck from 'round here askin' questions. He's in New York," said GQ.

"You're a lyin' bitch. I think you killed him, because I seen you wearin' his jewels and shit. That's okay . . . ." Lisa pulled out a pocket size camera and started taking pictures of the SB Crew.

"What the fuck do you think you doin' wit that camera?" asked GQ.

"Who the fuck you talkin' to? You fight like a bitch anyway. How you think you gonna run yo own crew? You pooh ass—"

Before Lisa could say another word, GQ brook loose from Travis, raised her left fist, and come down hard on Lisa's face like a flash of lightning. This action caused Lisa to go down on one knee.

"Cap, throw her the hell out of here and get that camera."

Cap picked Lisa up and carried her to the door.

"GQ, open the door," said Cap.

When GQ opened the door, Cap threw Lisa's ass down the steps. He snatched the camera out of Lisa's hand and slammed it on the ground, causing it to brake into little pieces. Cap didn't like GQ getting him involved in cleaning up her dirty work.

Hours later Travis and Cap left the crib. GQ told Travis that she wanted to stay at the house with Homicide in order to protect all of the goods. Homicide couldn't ascertain Bashi's friends from Bashi's enemies. He was going to get to the bottom of the disappearance. Infiltrating was the only thing on Homicide's mind.

The next morning Homicide was disturbed out of his sleep by the sound of the front door to the crib closing. Any strange movement or sound would wake him up instantly. He looked out of the window and saw GQ getting into the Jetta. Homicide went to take a shower and carried the .38 in the shower with him. Then he put on some clothes and went downstairs to get a pair of rubber gloves from under the kitchen sink. He was glad that GQ was gone so that he could check out Bashi's bedroom without interruption.

Everything was still untouched. He went into Bashi's bathroom and saw that things were spotless. The linen closet and underneath the cabinets were empty. *"If Bashi was comin' back from out of town, why was his bathroom cleaned out like this?"*

Homicide proceeded back into the bedroom where he saw that the closet door had a dent. About head level, there was a smudge of dried blood. With the gloves on, he pulled open the closet door; and Bashi's clothes were still hanging neatly.

Air fresheners were in different places of the bedroom, as if someone were trying to cover up a stench. The smell of bleach nearly made Homicide nauseous. The bed had no sheets. The room looked as if it had been vacant for some time. The biggest thing that recaptured his attention was the 7 foot long and 4 foot wide piece of carpet that was cut out of the floor in front of the bedroom door. As he looked on the walls, he could see discoloration of the paint in certain spots.

He tried to piece together what could have happened. *"There must have been a struggle. Bashi and the intruder must have fought, causin' one of them to be pushed hard into the closet door. Then there must have been some type of weapon that caused one of them to be killed on the bed. It couldn't have been a knife, because Bashi or the intruder cleaned the walls. So, it had to have been a gun to project blood in that pattern. Now why was the carpet missin'? Maybe the carpet was used to wrap a body up. GQ has Bashi's Jetta and Bronco. Lisa says she saw GQ with Bashi's jewelry. The dog is missing. Plus the light was out in the—"*

"Yo Homicide! You ready?!" shouted GQ from downstairs.

"Yeah, gimme a few minutes."

CHAPTER 23

Homicide knew this could be his last ride; however, he made sure he had his heater. They were going to see Maya, Bashi's sister. Homicide owed it to Bashi's family to find out the truth, because Bashi did a lot of great things to include giving Homicide a home off of the streets.

Once they arrived at Conshohocken, GQ parked the Jetta four blocks away from the park, where the meeting was to go down. As they were walking, Homicide asked, "GQ, you want me to tell Maya that Bashi sent you the money from New York to bail me out of jail?" Homicide wanted to see if GQ would go along with the lie, which might also mean that she would be untruthful about Bashi's disappearance.

"Yeah, you tell her Bashi sent money for you."

When Maya saw Homicide walking with GQ, Maya's eyes lit up with joy. She was elated to see Homicide. Maya gave him a hug and asked, "When you get out?"

"I got out last night. Bashi sent money for me."

Maya started talking with GQ, so Homicide walked away. Within 10 minutes, Homicide could see the anger in Maya's eyes. As GQ walked back to the car, Maya waved goodbye to Homicide. He felt like someone had hit him in his gut. This strengthened Homicide's resolve to find out what happened to Bashi.

Their ride back to Philly was very quiet. GQ dropped Homicide off at the crib. When Homicide went into the house, he had his hand on his heater just in case the intruder was inside. Then he saw that Travis and Cap were sitting in the living room. There was a knock; and Homicide opened the front door.

"Yo, where's Bashi? Somebody betta tell me somethin'," demanded the I.D. guy, who gave Homicide the name Holland.

"Homey, who the fuck you think you talkin' to?" asked Travis.

"Why did GQ want an I.D. with Bashi's name and birth date? . . . Homicide, when did you get out of jail?"

Homicide pulled out his heater and grabbed the I.D. guy, who was already looking very nervous. Homicide put the barrel of the gun to the I.D. guy's head and said, "Muthafucka, don't come 'round here askin' questions. Now get the fuck out of here; and don't come back, you pussy ass bitch." As Homicide was talking to him, Homicide pushed the I.D. guy out of the house. In all actuality, Homicide was trying to save the I.D. guy from getting hurt by Travis.

As Homicide turned back into the living room, Homicide felt there was something really wrong with the SB Crew; and he needed just a little more information. Just as Homicide was going to ask Travis more questions about the duplicate I.D., GQ came to take the Crew out for some grub. Homicide decided to stay at the crib, because things were starting to come together, piece by piece.

Now that they were gone, Homicide had time alone to think. *"GQ had stepped into the garage. What did she do that for?"* Homicide went outside and jumped over the fence. When Homicide stepped into the garage, he saw nothing but green trash bags. He started to turn and leave; but something caught his attention? He saw an object underneath a few trash bags. *"That's the same sheet that was on Bashi's bed the morning that I was arrested."* He didn't pay that much attention. After all, it was just a sheet. Homicide couldn't stay in there long because the flies were getting on his nerves. So he pushed on and went to the salon where Tammy worked.

"Is Tammy here?"

"Yes, her station is downstairs," said the salon receptionist.

When Homicide was in the basement, he saw five stations, which were all full.

"Excuse me. Which one of you is Tammy?"

This nice looking skimmie said, "That's me." Tammy had alluring black eyes, a snazzy short hair cut, and a bad ass body.

"Damn you fine. I'm Homicide, but you can call me Teco."

"You look nothin' like I thought you would," said Tammy.

"And how's that?"

"You know, the name Homicide makes me think of some dude sporting huge tattoos and a scar on his face with an evil look."

"So now that I don't look the part, what do you think?"

She raised her right eye brow and smiled at him. "Have you found out anything thus far?" asked Tammy.

"No, I haven't; but I know that somethin' is wrong with this new crew. Just gimme a few more hours."

"Okay, you keep me posted."

Homicide left the salon and went back to the SB Crib to pack his things. There was no more information he was going to gather by staying there. He was giving serious thought about calling the police. After Homicide entered the crib, he went back into Bashi's bedroom to check it out one more time. Homicide stared at the bed.

"Whatcha doin' in here?" asked Travis, who scared the shit out of Homicide. Travis came to the door and blocked Homicide in the room.

"Yo homie, you betta check yo'self. Mind yo business before I do it for you," said Homicide, who pushed Travis out of the way.

Homicide went to his bedroom to pack his shit. Where was Homicide going to live now? His family had moved to the D.C. area. He needed to talk with Tammy again before he left town.

As Homicide was walking out of the house, he remembered, *"Oh yeah, maybe the sheets in the garage were the last ones on Bashi's bed after all."* Homicide jumped the fence once more. He went into the garage and pulled the sheet from under the trash bags. What he saw next almost made him vomit. There was the carpet from Bashi's room and sticking out was a decaying hand.

"Oh shit! Those muthafuckas!" He quickly got out of there and hit the fence. He tried to get around to the shop as fast as he could to tell Tammy what he discovered. Once Homicide was in the shop he asked out of breath, "Is she downstairs?"

"Yes," said the salon receptionist.

He ran down the basement stairs; and as he hit the last step, he saw GQ sitting in Tammy's chair.

"Yo, wassup Homicide? Whatcha doin' 'round this joint?" asked GQ. The first thing Homicide did was put his hand on his heater. As he did so, he realized that the gun wasn't there. He had left it at the crib. As GQ saw that Homicide didn't have his heater, a big smile came over her face.

"I'm just chillin'. I came to ask Tammy if she wants to go to lunch," said Homicide.

Tammy had a worried look on her face. GQ was having the front of her hair dyed blond and getting her hair cut into a fade, almost making GQ look like a dude.

"Homicide, I need you to ride wit me after Tammy is finished," said GQ.

Homicide was thinking of a way to get away from GQ; however, it was too late. Tammy passed GQ the hand mirror to show GQ the new hair cut. Then GQ stood up and said, "Let's roll."

"Yo, go ahead to the car. I need to give Tammy somethin'."

"Hurry up homey," said GQ, who went up the salon stairs.

Homicide whispered to Tammy, "I think Bashi's body is in the garage at the crib. I think GQ killed him." Tammy gasped; and Homicide covered her mouth. Homicide continued to say, "Don't cry. You gotta hold it together for me until I get out of the salon. My mother lives in D.C. Here is her name and digits. Call my mom; tell her what I seen and that I'm with GQ now. Do you have Maya's number?"

"Yeah, it's right here. Bashi gave it to me after we hooked up." Tears started to fall down Tammy's face. Homicide began to wipe them away with his thumb.

"Be strong for Bashi," said Homicide, as he kissed Tammy on the forehead.

"Be careful Homicide," said Tammy.

When Homicide hit the top step to the salon's first floor, he didn't see GQ. He opened the glass door to the salon and the bell on the door startled him. He looked down the street and saw that GQ was already in the Jetta waiting for him.

"Yo, let's go grab somethin' to eat. First, I gotta go back to the crib and get some dough," said GQ.

"I'm not hungry," said Homicide.

"Well, I am. After I get the dough, let's go to the food court at Cheltonham Mall."

When they pulled up at the crib, GQ went into the house. This was Homicide's opportunity to grab his heater from the front fender of Bashi's Bronco. As he sat back down in the passenger's seat and closed the door to the Jetta, GQ came out of the house. Fortunately, she didn't see him make his move.

They arrived at the mall. After GQ sat down at a table in the food court with her tray of Chinese cuisine, her pager went off. She showed Homicide the number, 91191177729777911, which kept displaying back to back.

"Go check this number for me," said GQ.

She gave Homicide the pager. He walked around the corner of the food court to the pay phones. He went back to GQ and said, "No one answered."

Just as he said this, the pager went off again with the same number. GQ was almost finished eating. Once she was done, they walked to the bank of phones; and GQ called the number.

"Yo, who's this?" The person on the other end said something to GQ that caused her to give Homicide a look that could have killed Homicide, if looks could kill. "A'right, I'm already at Cheltonham Mall. He's not packin'," said GQ. Then she turned to Homicide and said, "What the fuck have you done?"

"What the fuck are you talkin' 'bout?"

"You know, you punk ass. Let's go meet Travis D. and Cap at the front entrance."

As soon as Travis saw Homicide, Travis asked, "Homicide what the hell you tell yo mom 'bout there's a body in the house?"

"What the hell you talkin' 'bout?" asked Homicide.

"The police came to the SB Crib and said you called yo mom's in D.C. and told her that there was a body in the crib. I told them that they had false info, that we live in the crib too, and that Bashi is in New York. You lucky they didn't search the crib. We got mad drugs up in there," said Travis, who tried to swing on Homicide hoping to knock Homicide's ass out. That's when Homicide pulled the heater from under his shirt and pointed the gun at Travis in broad day light.

Just as Homicide did this, Travis, GQ, and Cap backed away from him.

"Homicide you not down wit us no more," said GQ.

Homicide walked backwards out of the mall, kept his eyes on them, and said, "That's cool wit me, 'cause you muthafuckas grimy."

Homicide hailed a cab to Fatboy's crib. "Is Fatboy here?" asked Homicide.

"Now you know his ass is in the basement," said Mr. G.

Homicide ran down the stairs. When he saw Fatboy, he said, "I need to use one of your dad's ladders."

"For what?" asked Fatboy.

"The crib is locked. I need to climb through the window and get my shit and other things. Are you down?" asked Homicide, who also briefed Fatboy on everything that occurred in the last 48 hours.

"Yeah, can I get some shit too?"

"That's up to you. Just stay out my way. We only have 10 minutes."

They carried the ladder to the SB crib. Once they stood the ladder up to Homicide's bedroom window, Homicide was the first one through the window. Homicide went straight to Bashi's room and grabbed some clothes. Then he went to GQ's bedroom and stuffed into his pockets the jewels that GQ had taken from Bashi, which included three gold rope necklaces and five rings. Homicide flipped GQ's mattress, which had a square cut in it. Homicide pulled the flap back. *This can't be all the loti and dope.* Homicide was disappointed. So he went to the safe, which was open and empty. The SB Crew never ran out of money, even though they were known to spend big and long. Homicide found a green duffle bag and put everything that he found into it.

"Yo, Fatboy, let's go."

"A'right. Look, when I get down, drop me the bags," said Fatboy. After they were on the sidewalk, Fatboy continued to say, "Yo Teco, where's the body?"

"In the garage."

They were ingenious on how they strapped the bags to the ladder in order to carry everything back to Fatboy's crib. They hoped that police weren't cruising the streets. Once they returned the ladder, Homicide went to catch the bus. He needed to stop at the pawn shop at Broad and Logan.

After entering into the pawn shop, Homicide said, "Hey, I need to pawn this stuff. What can I get for it all?" Homicide was very nervous. All he wanted to do was make it out of town.

"I'll give you $800," said the pawn shop owner.

"Okay, that's cool," said Homicide.

The owner gave Homicide the money; then Homicide went to catch the subway to the 30th Street Station. While he was on the subway train, the man on the loud speaker exclaimed, "30th Street Amtrak Station!" Homicide got off and went to the entrance. He could hear the Amtrak man announcing departures and arrivals. After he looked around, Homicide located the sign that read, "Ticket Purchase."

CHAPTER 24

Homicide joined the line and stood behind a woman who was burping a new born baby. Just as he was about to tell the mother that the baby had spit up on her shoulder, the Amtrak ticket counter clerk said, "Sir, I'll take you over here."

"He walked up to the window and said, "I need a one-way ticket to Washington, D.C."

"Will that be all sir?"

"Yes."

"That will be $55. Your train leaves from 35A in 45 minutes."

"Thank you M'am."

"Thank you for choosing Amtrak."

Homicide went to the McDonalds in the terminal to eat before he got onto the train. After he finished eating his Big Mac and fries, he was fiendishly craving a joint to calm his nerves. The weed that he took from GQ's room was at the bottom of the duffle bag. So he started taking the stuff out of the duffle bag, trying his best not to be noticed. Once he got a good size bud, he put the clothes back into the bag. He wanted to walk outside, but knew that he couldn't leave his bag beside a bench. Homicide found an empty wall locker and placed his things inside. Then he went towards the front exit. Just as he looked up, he stopped in his tracks and started to back up. *"What the fuck are they doin' here? How do they know that I'm here?"*

Homicide saw GQ and Travis; however, they never saw him. Homicide watched them for a few minutes and slipped out the side of the building, where workers had been doing construction on the Amtrak Station. He walked up two blocks to smoke his joint. *"How they know I'm here? Think . . . If I were lookin' for someone to leave town, where would I go to find them? That's right, the train station."* Homicide couldn't believe that GQ and Travis were that smart. He had to find a way to slip back into the station and down to track 35A.

Homicide retraced his tracks, hoping that he would not be seen by GQ or Travis. He grabbed his duffle bag. In order to reach track 35A, Homicide had to walk to the other side of the station. He looked around and saw that GQ was at one entrance and that Travis was standing at the other. At that moment, Homicide felt stuck. He positioned himself so that he could keep his eyes on both of them. As he observed GQ, he could see the bulge of her heater. Travis was too far away for Homicide to see if Travis was packing any heat.

Then the announcer said over the loud speaker, "All passengers for the train to Washington, D.C., the train is now boarding on track 35A. The train will be departing in 10 minutes."

A crowd of school students and seven military police were walking toward track 31B. Homicide seized the opportunity to get on the other side of the group. He walked between the military police and the students. GQ and Travis never saw Homicide. He rushed down the stairs almost knocking over some passengers. Once on the train, he sat in the back far right corner. As he pulled out a pack of Newports, the train started to move. *"I'm glad I made it out. Fuck them pussy ass bitches."* He pulled out the wad of money. Homicide counted $7,500. He knew that he had enough to get back on his feet and to start SB in D.C.

◊◊◊◊◊

Tammy and Maya had been talking on the phone ever since Homicide left the shop. Maya was trying to get Tammy to calm down so that she could understand what Tammy was saying.

"Girl, what was the last thing Homicide told you?" asked Maya.

"He said somethin' 'bout a body at the SB Crib and to call his mother for him. He was very scared, because I could hear it in his voice." Tammy couldn't bear to tell Maya that Homicide thought the body was Bashi. Tears were streaming down Tammy's face.

"Do you know where Homicide is now?"

"No, the last time I seen him was when him and GQ were here in the shop."

"Do you think?—"

"Don't. We have no idea and we can't start guessing now."

"Do you have Homicide's mother's number?"

"Yes, hold on. Let me find it." Tammy put the phone down and went to get the piece of paper that Homicide gave her. "Are you still there?" asked Tammy.

"Yeah," said Maya.

"Okay. It's 907-3854"

"Thanks Tammy. If you hear from Homicide tell him to call me, please."

After hours of trying to reach Homicide's mother, Maya tried the number again. The phone rang five times before a man picked up the phone and said, "Hello."

"Yes, this is Mujaheed Bashi Fiten's sister, Maya. I'm looking for Homicide or his mother. Is either one of them in?" There was a long pause of silence on the phone. Maya asked, "Hello. Hello. Are you still there?"

"Yes, I'm still here. This is Homicide. Maya, you have to call me Teco when you call the house." There was another pause of silence.

"Teco, I'm glad I found you. Can you tell me what you know 'bout my brutha? Bashi didn't bail you out. I know that you got out of jail on O.R., 'cause I checked. So I need you to be straight wit me."

Homicide told Maya everything that he heard and what he discovered over his first 48 hours out of jail. He explained to her why he told her that Bashi had sent the money to bail him out. He could hear the sobs over the telephone.

Maya tried to speak clearly and asked, "Now Teco, are you sure 'bout the body in the garage?"

"Yes, I wouldn't lie to you 'bout that. Bashi was the one who took me off of the streets."

"A'right, I'll give you a call later, when I get more information."

Maya hung up the phone and called the police to report her brother missing. She conveyed to the police what Teco had told her. Though she didn't want to hear the news, Maya felt in her spirit that her brother's body would be found. Within 2 hours, the sergeant from the Broad and Olney 33rd precinct called Maya and said, "M'am, this is Sergeant Duncan. I'm sorry to say that we found nothing at that address."

"Are you sure?" asked Maya.

"M'am, we sent officers out there twice."

"Why didn't you just go into the house and look? Why didn't you search the garage?"

"M'am, we don't have a search warrant. We just can't burst into someone's house without probable cause." Maya was getting more and more hysterical and hung up on the officer without saying goodbye. She composed herself and then called Teco again.

"Hello."

"Yes, may I speak with Teco?"

"This is me. Wassup Maya?"

"The police said they went over to the house and nothing was wrong. Are you sure that you saw a body?"

"Yes, I'm very sure."

"Can you tell my brutha, Basil, what you told me?"

"Okay, put him on."

"Hello Homicide, this is Basil. What happened?" Homicide told Basil everything that he told Maya, to include that all evidence and motive pointed to GQ. He shared with Basil that GQ wanted her own Crew and was sporting Bashi's jewels; plus the money was missing.

Basil said, "Well, if this is what you seen, I'm goin' ova to the house myself and take Yusef wit me. We'll see if a body is there."

Basil and Yusef went to the SB Crib. They checked the front door to see if it was opened; however, the door was locked. They decided to jump the fence. Yusef went to see if the back door was opened. Basil saw that the garage door was still halfway opened as Homicide had described. So Basil went into the garage and paused when he saw the sheet.

"Yo Yusef, come in here. I think this is the sheet Homicide was talkin' 'bout. It smells like shit in here," said Basil.

"Yeah, that must be it. Let's see what's goin' down," said Yusef. Then Yusef pulled some of the trash bags from off of the pile to get to the sheet and shouted, "Oh shit! Oh Shit! What the fu—"

"No, No, No! I'm gonna kill that pussy muthafucka!" exclaimed Basil. Yusef grabbed Basil to calm him down, which was useless. "They killed my brutha man!" Tears were streaming down Basil's eyes.

"Come on. We need to call the po po," said Yusef. Yusef and Basil hopped back over the fence in order to call the police. As they were pacing on the sidewalk in front of the house, sirens could be heard from all over the area.

"Are you the ones who called the police?" asked an officer.

"Yeah, we did," said Yusef.

"What's the problem here?" asked the officer.

Basil lost it and said, "My brutha has been murdered! His body is in the muthafuckin' garage. You pussies came here earlier and didn't find shit. If you muthafuckas had done your job, you would have found my brutha . . . ." Basil bent over and vomited on the sidewalk.

"Sir, please calm down. Where's the body?"

"In the garage in a sheet under the trash," said Yusef.

"Sir, do you have any idea who would have done this?"

"Yes, her muthafuckin' name is Gail Indigo Que. You betta find that bitch before I get to her," said Basil.

The police officer went into his trunk and pulled out a pair of bolt cutters for the lock on the fence. Detectives entered the garage and came out wearing medical face masks over their noses. One police officer put up yellow crime scene tape around the perimeter. The detectives asked Basil and Yusef question after question. Another officer pulled out a handheld and said, "This is an A.P.B. for murder suspect, Gail Indigo Que, a.k.a. GQ. She was last seen in a blue Jetta with license plate number FZ-1673. Suspect is a black female, 5'11, slim build, short blond hair, and hazel eyes. Please proceed with caution. Suspect may be armed and dangerous."

◊◊◊◊◊

Two days later, GQ was spotted driving the Jetta and making an illegal lane change in North Philly on Broad Street. The police car, which was at the corner of Joe Frazier's Boxing Gym on Summerset Street, pulled out and turned on the lights. The police siren made a loud "Whoop! Whoop!" sound to give GQ the warning to pull over. However, GQ did the opposite. When she reached Lehigh Avenue, she took a hard right going 50 mph.

"This is patrol unit 919 in pursuit of a blue Jetta."

"919 what is your location?"

"I'm on Lehigh going west in the direction of Fairmont Park."

"What's the tag number unit 919?" Before the officer responded he saw two more police cars joining in the pursuit.

"F as in Frank, Z as in Zebra, 1-6-7-3."

GQ was weaving through cars going all over to the other side of the road.

"All units in pursuit of the blue Jetta tag number FZ-1673, the driver is a possible murder suspect; so proceed with caution. She may be armed and dangerous," said the radio dispatcher.

As GQ drove towards Fairmont Park, she tried to make a left turn by the 33rd street SEPTA Bus Station. She hit a mail box and ended flipping the Jetta five times and landing in the park.

"Oh shit!" said the police officer.

As all of the civilian cars pulled over, the police circled the Jetta. "This is 919. We need a rescue team at 33rd Street." The police ran on foot over to the car with their guns drawn and shouted, "Don't move! Don't you move!" However, GQ was knocked unconscious. As soon as the rescue team arrived, they were able to get GQ out of the car. The EMT took her to St. Joseph Medical Hospital on 19th and Girade Avenue.

◊◊◊◊◊

GQ was in critical condition for 2 weeks. As she regained consciousness in her private hospital room, she kept drifting in and out due to the medication for severe pain. In a dream state, visions of Bashi kept coming into her mind. GQ repeated over and over, "Why? Why? Why?"

The black male nurse, who was in the room taking GQ's vital signs, looked down upon her. This was the first time he noticed that GQ was pretty. The nurse placed his hand on GQ's shoulder and said, "Baby girl, time heals all wounds."

GQ's eyes opened; and the nurse jumped back, because GQ's eyes were as brilliant as a Siamese cat. He had never seen a black woman's eyes the color of deep almond-blue.

GQ asked, "May I have some water? I'm sorry. What's yo name?"

"I'm Nurse Collins. I apologize for being somewhat taken aback. Your eyes . . . Your eyes are stunning."

"May I get the water now?"

"Sure."

Before Nurse Collins could return, GQ fell asleep again.

Bashi was standing in his bedroom at the SB Crib. Intruders walked into his room. Bashi looked to his right at the .38, which was on his night stand. Bashi briefly took his eyes off of this dude, who struck Bashi with a solid punch to Bashi's jaw. This threw Bashi into the closet door. As Bashi tried to get up, a female, who was also in the room, kicked Bashi in the ribs, sending Bashi back onto the floor. "You think you so tough runnin' wit that punk ass wanna be thug?"

Bashi was a diehard type gangsta. With all his might, Bashi leapt for the gun. However, the female grabbed the .38 and shot Bashi. Pow! As Bashi fell down, he looked at the shooter and said, "Why? Why?"

GQ came back into consciousness in a cold sweat and realized that she was still in the hospital bed. Nurse Collins was taking her vital signs and reached to give GQ the water.

"Here, this might make you feel a little better," said Nurse Collins.

"How long have I been here?" asked GQ.

"Two weeks."

"Am I gonna be able to walk again?"

"Let me go page the doctor and he will speak with you." As Nurse Collins left the room, GQ continued to dream.

Neither of the killers gave Bashi a response. The female shot Bashi 4 more times feeling no remorse. Pow! Pow! Pow! Pow! The last shot hit Bashi in the head, spraying blood all over the walls and on the accomplice, who said, "Shit, I didn't want this fool's blood on me."

"You should have moved out the way. Come on help me put him in the tub."

"Why you puttin' him in the tub?"

159

"He's still alive. Let's keep him there until he's dead."

"You lost yo damn mind. Let's wrap this punk and dump his ass."

"No, we will leave and come back when we know fo sho that he's dead."

They grabbed Bashi by the feet and shoulders. "On 3, 1 . . . 2 . . . 3 . . . ." They lifted the body and carried it to the tub in Bashi's bathroom. Then they left the SB Crib.

The doctor walked into the room and asked, "Ms. Que, Ms. Que, can you hear me?" GQ opened her eyes, which now appeared hazel in color. The doctor continued to say, "You are going to be fine. We will keep you on pain medicine and start you on physical therapy if necessary. Can you wiggle your toes? I have ordered x-rays."

GQ couldn't respond and drifted back into the dream.

When they walked back into the SB Crib, there was a very foul stench in the air.

"You smell that shit?"

As they went upstairs the smell became much stronger. They entered the room with caution. While they went into the bathroom, neither touched anything. Bashi's lifeless body was lying in the tub with blood under it.

"Grab the sheets off the bed and spread it out on the floor."

"No let's lay the body on the floor and cut out some carpet to roll him in; then we can wrap the sheets 'round it."

"Damn he is heavy as shit."

They had a problem lifting the carpet with Bashi's body inside; so they dragged the carpet down the steps. Each time it went to the next step, a loud thumping noise could be heard throughout the house. Then they proceeded to dispose of the body as if it were trash.

GQ sat up in the bed in a panic. Sweat was coming down her forehead and her breathing was irregular. *"I gotta get outta here. I need to find Homicide."*

Nurse Collins reentered the room and asked, "You alright? Do you need some more water? Where does it hurt?"

"I'll be fine. I can wiggle my toes."

Then a female x-ray technician came into the room to take GQ for x-rays. GQ noticed that there were no police officers posted on any of the hospital doors. After the x-ray, the technician turned the lights out. Unexpectedly GQ jumped up and grabbed the technician around her neck and said, "Gimme the muthafuckin' keys to the elevator!"

"Please don't hurt me." The x-ray technician gave GQ the key ring; and GQ tied her up.

GQ limped down the hall to the elevator and used the key to activate the down button. Just as she stepped out of the elevator on the ground floor, a police officer was running down the hall and shouted, "Freeze! Stay right there. Don't move!" People were all around and the officer continued to say, "Everyone, get down! Get down!"

GQ took advantage of the crowd and ran out of the hospital toward Richard Allen projects. The same police officer was right behind her. Then a SEPTA bus came and separated them. The police had lost GQ; and that wasn't good. Police cars were all over the place. GQ had the lead on them. Once she got into the projects, she went to the closest building. She approached the first apartment door and kicked it open. Then she knocked out the light in the ceiling. GQ didn't see that the elderly woman, who lived in the house, ran into the bathroom with the cordless phone.

"911, how may I help you?"

"Someone just kicked my door in; and I ran into the bathroom."

"M'am, where do you stay?"

"I stay in Richard Allen Building 57-B.

"M'am stay away from the door. Stay in the bathroom. We are sending someone over right now."

A local cop, walking the beat in the neighborhood, heard the call over the police radio and said, "This is 1974 on foot patrol in the vicinity."

"1974 proceed with caution; the suspect may be armed and dangerous."

As the officer went inside the building, GQ could hear the cop walking by the door. She positioned herself behind the door waiting for the officer to come into the house. The officer pulled out his service revolver and said, "If you're in there, you need to come out right now, with your hands up."

There was no response. The police officer saw the door was ajar and entered the room with his gun drawn. GQ lunged for the officer's gun. The officer pulled the gun back trying his best not to let go. GQ seemed to be getting the best of the cop. She hit him in the face. They struggled for the gun and simultaneously fell onto the floor. The next sound the elderly woman heard was one loud shot from the officer's revolver. Pow!

CHAPTER 25

Even though Teco lived with his mother in Washington, D.C., he still had the Philly mindset. SB was still in his heart. He found a location for some potential work from a local dealer in Southeast D.C. The street life in the D.C. area was very different from Philly. This part of the streets was about selling that hard crack. On his way to the projects in D.C., Teco had to remember where he was and how he got there, so that he could quickly get out if necessary. Once he was in the hood, he could see that things were slower here. This dude was running to cars; so Teco saw this as a great opportunity to step to him.

"Yo, where can I get some major work?" asked Teco.

"Who the fuck you callin' Yo?" asked the dude. Teco knew that he didn't need any trouble; therefore, he didn't respond. The dude continued to say, "You need somethin' or what?"

"Yeah, I need some weight," said Teco.

"Who the fuck are you?"

"I'm from Philly. Are you the man to deal wit?"

"No, but come wit me."

"Hold up. You think I'm suppose to just roll wit you? Hell no. It don't work like that," said Teco.

"I'm takin' you to the pool hall ova there."

When Teco went into the building, he saw a tall dude shooting pool. This dude had all of his young gorillas around him. Teco could tell that most of them were packing heat. This dude pointed to a table in the back of the room and said, "Youngen, you can have a seat ova there." Teco sat with his back to the wall and with his hand under his shirt. The same dude came over to Teco and asked, "Wassup Youngen? I'm Big R.E. Who you?"

"I'm Teco."

"Where you from Teco?"

"West Philly."

"You here for good?"

"Well, that all depends on if the loti is right."

"Where you stay?"

"I think you gettin' too personal homey. You either have what I need or you don't."

"What do you need?"

"½ ounce of some raw."

"Do you boil yo own?"

"What do you mean boil my own?" asked Teco.

"All we sell out here is that hard rock."

"You talkin' 'bout rock as in crack?"

"Yeah, if you want to call it that." Teco knew he had no knowledge about crack and that he was out of his league. R.E. continued to say, "Who you work for?"

"I don't work for nobody."

"Well look. When you need some work come back and see me. I'll front you whateva you need; but it will only be hard."

The next day Teco was watching a television program called City Under Siege. He saw how bodies were coming up dead on the streets; and he was trying to put this life behind him. The police were busting local drug houses all over the D.C. and Maryland area. Teco knew that this wasn't where he wanted to due his SB business.

So he decided to change careers and went to look for a job. The first place he went to was a children's clothing store called "Clothing for Kids by Melvin." He was hired without experience.

As Teco returned from work and entered his mother's crib, the phone was ringing. "Hello."

"Can I speak with Teco?"

"Wassup Maya?"

"The detectives, who are on Bashi's case, would like to talk with you. Is it okay if I give them yo number?"

"I don't know. I really want to put that behind me."

"Can you do this for Bashi? Remember, you are fam to us."

164

Teco paused for a few seconds and said, "A'right. I'll talk wit them."

"Thank you so so much."

Within an hour, Teco's phone rang again. "Hello."

"May I speak with Teco Jackson?"

"Speaking. Who am I speaking wit?"

"This is Detective Walker from the 33rd Precinct."

"Yes, how can I help you?"

"I would like to talk to you about Mujaheed Bashi Fiten. I think you call him Bashi."

Teco repeated the facts he knew to the detective. Then the detective said, "Can my partner and I come to D.C. and record your statement? You have put together the missing pieces for our case."

"Sure, I can give you a statement. When are you coming?"

"We would like to come in two days. Is that fine with you?"

"Yes, I just need to let my job know the time so that I can get off of work." Teco gave them the address and the directions on how to find him.

"Okay, we'll see you then. Thank you, Teco."

Two days later, Detective Walker and Detective Robinson arrived to D.C. at 1:00pm. They called Teco from the local police station to make sure that he was home before they came over. After the brief conversation, Teco was nervous about the meeting. He put on a white shirt, black tie, and black dress pants.

After the Detective knocked on the door, a tall strikingly beautiful light-skinned woman opened the door and asked, "May I help you?"

"Yes M'am, we are detectives from Philadelphia; and we set up a meeting with Teco Jackson. Is he available?" asked Detective Walker.

"Yes, just a minute," said Teco's mother.

Before Teco reached the door, he adjusted his tie. There stood two well built black men in two piece suits. Teco could see their guns bulging from their sides. One Detective had a large folder in his hands.

"Are you Teco?"

"Yes, that's me. Come in. Would you like anything to drink?"

"No, thank you. I'm Detective Walker and this is Detective Robinson."

"I'm Teco Jackson, a.k.a. Homicide." The two detectives laughed, because Teco didn't look like a killer.

Detective Walker asked, "Look, can you tell us what happened?"

"I only can tell you what I know."

"Okay, that is all we would like to hear."

"Do you mind if we put this on tape?"

"No, that's fine wit me."

Detective Robinson took out a small tape recorder and said, "When we press record, we will ask you some questions."

"Testing. Testing. This is Detective Walker and Detective Robinson from the 33rd Precinct in Philadelphia, PA. We're at the home of Teco Jackson, a.k.a. Homicide. We're interviewing him about the death of Mujaheed Bashi Fiten, Case File Number FITEN01-HOM."

Teco started in the beginning from the time he first met Bashi and went into details about his role in SB. Then he told them about the 48 hour search for Bashi and how all evidence seemed to point to GQ. This is when Detective Robinson pulled out the pictures from the crime scene and showed Teco where Bashi was shot.

Detective Walker said, "GQ was in a high speed chase, escaped from the hospital, and was shot by a police officer in a Richard Allen apartment."

◊◊◊◊◊

Two Years Later

◊◊◊◊◊

The sun warmed Teco's face as he walked out of the D.C. jail. He found it hard to put Bashi's death behind him. Bashi was not only a friend, but also a strong male figure. Without Bashi providing direction and security, Teco started doing his old thing of stealing Johnnies and finding refuge in the homes of women. He was glad to be released from jail. As he caught the Metrobus, he was wondering if his girlfriend, Rasheeda Igrubia, was at home. Because they were a couple, Rasheeda had given Teco a key to her apartment; and he could hardly wait to see her again. She and Teco met two years ago when Teco was working at the children's store.

Teco sat back on the bus seat and remembered when he first saw Rasheeda. She walked into the store wearing a fitted t-shirt and tight blue jeans. Her brown hair was shoulder length and bounced as she walked. Her facial dimples along with her bright white teeth made an entire room light up. Rasheeda reminded Teco of Rhonda. They had mind blowing sex. Rasheeda found him to be very charming; and because she lived alone, she liked the security Teco brought into her life. Teco had done a good job of hiding his past life in Philly from her.

As Teco walked up to Rasheeda's apartment, the teenage girl who lived down stairs walked up to Teco and said, "Teco, Teco, this detective was lookin' for you. He came 'round two times."

"When was this?"

"Last night."

"Okay, thanks."

Teco knew that he had done a lot of things and thought this to be one of law enforcement's ways of trying to knock him off. He thought it was best to pack his clothes and to leave Rasheeda. When he went up to the apartment, there was a white card in the door. Teco pulled the card out and on the back it read, "This is Detective Hunter from the Metropolitan Police Department Headquarters. Give me a call. This is very important."

Teco unlocked the door to Rasheeda's apartment. She was no where to be found. He sat on the couch for a few minutes, picked up the phone, and dialed the number on the card.

"Detective Hunter, how may I help you?"

"Yes sir, this is Teco Jackson."

"Teco, I know all about your past and that you just got out of jail today for auto theft."

"What do you want from me? I'm clean."

"I spoke with the District Attorney's office in Philadelphia. They would like for you to call them. The number is 467-5892. Ask for Peter Brown. He is the District Attorney."

"A'right. Is that all?"

"Oh yeah. One more thing. Stay out of trouble."

As Teco hung up the phone, Rasheeda walked into the apartment. Teco decided that this was going to be the best time to tell her about what happened with SB and that he was once known as Homicide.

While they sat and stared into each other's eyes, she broke their eye contact and said, "Well Teco, are you gonna call the man?"

"Yeah, hand me the phone." While Teco dialed, Rasheeda gave him a supportive smile.

"Hello. Thanks for calling the Philadelphia Superior Court District Attorney's office. How may I direct your call?"

"Mr. Peter Brown, please." Teco heard elevator music on the line.

"Peter Brown."

"Yes, this is Teco Jackson."

"Teco! I've been trying to find you for a long time. I need you to listen to me real good. We have Gail Indigo Que, a.k.a. GQ, on trial for the murder of Bashi. You're the key witness. Without your testimony, we don't have a case. I will send a car to get you and will pay for your hotel. The department gives you $20 each day and takes care of your meals. When the trial is over, we will send you back to D.C. on Amtrak. Will you be a state's witness?"

"Yes, I'll do it for Bashi's family."

"Good. I'll set it up and have two undercover agents, who have been working the case, to come pick you up tomorrow. I'll call you in the morning."

Teco hung up the phone and told Rasheeda what was going down.

"Baby, how long will you be gone?" asked Rasheeda.

"Until the trial is ova."

"Will you be safe?"

"Yeah, no one knows that I'm comin' into town but the D.A. I need to go pick out a suit." Teco finally felt that there might be some resolution to this whole ordeal. *"I'll get GQ's ass now. She's not expecting this."*

"You go take a shower. I'll go pack your bag," said Rasheeda.

The next morning, D.A. Peter Brown called Teco and said, "Hello Teco, are you ready?"

"Yes sir," said Teco.

"Alright, two agents should be there at noon today to pick you up from your girlfriend's place."

"Okay, I'll see you at the courthouse in the morning."

"No, I'm having them to bring you to my office first. I need you to sign some papers."

"What papers?"

"Just some papers stating that you did show up."

"Okay, that's cool."

At 12:30 that afternoon, an undercover agent drove up to Rasheeda's crib. His partner got out of the car and knocked on the door. When Teco answered the door, the agent asked, "Are you Teco Jackson?"

"Yeah, wassup?"

"Are you ready to go?"

"Yes, let me get my things."

"I'll be in the car."

CHAPTER 26

Once Teco got into the backseat of the car, the two undercover agents turned around to greet him.

"I'm Agent James."

"I'm Agent Rentson. Just sit back and enjoy your free trip."

"A'right," said Teco.

When Teco woke up, he was looking at the tall buildings in Center City. He was back in Philly. Teco wondered how Fatboy was doing. He really missed hanging out with his homey.

"We're here," said Teco.

"Yep, our orders are to take you to your hotel and see you to your room," said Agent James. They took him to a hotel in Chinatown. The Front Desk Clerk checked Teco into a king size smoking room and gave him the key.

"Tonight all we ask is that you stay in your room," said Agent Rentson.

In room number 825, Teco was sitting with no weed and no woman. He slouched in the chair with his left elbow on the table and his left hand holding up his head. Reality hit him square in the face. The D.A. was dependent on his testimony. With no appetite, he was tired of rehearsing every plausible answer to GQ's defense attorney's potential questions. The stress was exhausting. He fell asleep in the chair; however, when he woke up the next morning, he was lying on top of the bedspread. Teco had to hurry up and shower or he would be late for court.

He put on his blue suit, a white shirt, and a fly ass paisley tie. Dapper all the way around, Teco put on a pair of nice Polo sunglasses, which gave him a very aristocratic appearance. He looked in the bathroom mirror and thought about what Bashi had once said. *"You leave as a*

Crew, come back as a Crew, and you suffer as a Crew." Teco wondered, if he had worked out his conflict with GQ, would things have turned out differently. Then he heard a knock on the hotel room door.

When he reached the D.A.'s office, Teco was told to have a seat in the waiting area. The 1970's style office furniture was uncomfortable. The white tiled floors were polished so well that they looked wet. Teco picked up The Philadelphia Inquirer, which was on the coffee table. There was no mention of the trial on the front page. Just as he turned to the Entertainment section, a distinguished white man, who had a blond crew cut, extended his hand and said, "Hello, I'm Peter Brown." District Attorney Brown was impressed by the firmness of Teco's handshake. Then he continued to say, "Please follow me to my office."

They walked down a long hall to a large corner office with a magnificent view. D.A. Brown said, "Have a seat please." He explained to Teco what would be taking place in court. Several people weren't expecting Teco to show up, which was the other reason D.A. Brown didn't want him to go to the courthouse first. Then D.A. Brown pulled out the paperwork and put an "X" by the line, where Teco was to sign stating that he appeared in court as a state's witness.

When Teco went to the courthouse, Agent James and Agent Rentson were with him. One was on each side; and D.A. Brown was in front of him. Teco felt like a big time celebrity. As he walked down the hall in the courthouse, he could hear someone from Bashi's family ask, "Is that Homicide?"

"I don't know. It looks like him," said Basil.

"He looks very different than before."

"Yes, that's him," said Basil. Bashi's family stopped Teco, a.k.a. Homicide, and gave him hugs. Everyone thanked him for coming.

Then the D.A. took Teco to a room that was for witnesses only. Teco was shocked to see that Lisa Turner was also there as a witness. D.A. Brown needed Lisa's testimony in regards to the day that she confronted GQ about Bashi's jewelry. Waiting to testify made for a long day. Teco was never called to take the stand. When the day ended, D.A. Brown came to the witness room and directed Teco and Lisa to go back to the hotel.

"Teco, what hotel do they have you in?" asked Lisa.

"The one in Chinatown."

"Me too."

"Do you want to walk together," asked Teco.

"Yeah, that will be cool. I'm game. What are—"

"You are not to talk about the case. Period," said D.A. Brown.

Lisa continued to say, "What are you doing later?"

"Nothin'. Why you ask, slim?" asked Teco.

"You'll see." Teco and Lisa walked several blocks while talking about the night they met at the After Midnight Club.

"What were you and Sonya thinkin' when you put on those t-shirts wit yo names on it?" asked Teco.

"Got us to the VIP table; didn't it?" Teco just laughed.

As they both got onto the hotel elevator, Lisa pressed the 6th floor and Teco pressed the 8th floor. They were glad to be away from all of the officers and attorneys.

"Do you still smoke weed?" asked Lisa.

"Sho yo right. Why? Wassup?" asked Teco.

"I have some for me. If you want some, come by later. My room number is 610."

"Okay, I'll think 'bout that."

Teco took a hot shower and put on some comfortable black satin lounging pants as well as a white tank top. Teco looked at his physique in the mirror. Bashi's family was right. He did look different. He was much more muscular than when he lived in Philly years ago. Teco could see that the weight lifting in the D.C. jail really had paid off.

He picked up his Newports and grabbed his room key. On the way to Lisa's room, he picked up some ice. Teco had real plans on his mind for Lisa and wanted her to remember this night. He knocked on door 610.

"Who is it?" asked Lisa.

"She knows damn well who it is." In a deep sexy voice he said, "It's Teco."

"Just a minute." She came to the door wearing a white terry robe.

"You must excuse me. I just got out of the shower." She invited him into the room, went into the bathroom alone, and shut the door. From the bathroom she said, "Teco, look under the pillow and roll us two or three joints."

"A'right, do you mind if I open the door to the balcony?"

"No, go ahead."

When she came out of the bathroom, Lisa had on a red laced halter babydoll sleeper. There was no denying what she wanted.

"So Lisa, where do you live now?"

"In Atlanta, Georgia. Where do you stay?"

"Washington, D.C."

They both sat in the white plastic chairs on the balcony and passed the joint back and forth. There were no lights on in the room; therefore, the only glow was from the night skies.

"Do you have anything to drink?" asked Teco.

"Yeah some Gin. Would you like some?" asked Lisa.

"Sure, if you don't mind."

Lisa looked at the bucket of ice and asked, "Why did you bring ice wit you?"

"You don't know?" asked Teco.

"No, tell me what I don't know."

"I can show you betta than I can tell you."

"Okay, you do that then." They looked at each other with enticing smiles.

As they smoked the weed, they both became relaxed with each other. Teco got bold and took off his tank top. He stood in front of Lisa and flexed his chest muscles. She liked his advances and she put her hands on his chest.

"Teco, dance for me."

"What? No . . . How 'bout you dance for me?"

"Come wit me back into the room and dance. Pleez."

Lisa turned the radio onto a jazz station; and Teco started to give her a private show. She liked the way his body moved effortless to the rhythm of the music. He was smooth as he came over to her and applied soft kisses down her neck. Then he picked her up and put her legs around his waist. Lisa was going with the flow of both the jazz sounds and Teco. With his hands on her round soft ass, Lisa let out a passionate moan. Then she whispered, "Oh Teecoo, I like the way you squeeze my ass. Baby, I've wanted you a long time." He let her slide down his body slowly as he put her down; and in that instant, the song ended. If she didn't know any better, she would have thought he danced professionally. He took her hand and walked her to the bed. As she lay down, Teco got a piece of ice and put it in his mouth. Then he blew in Lisa's ears. "Ooh, ohh, baby I like that," said Lisa as she reached to take off her red thong.

"No, let me undress you. You just enjoy this."

He went down on her to pull her sexy thong off. Then he came out of his satin lounge pants. He reached into his pocket to get the Trojan condoms. He pulled one out of the pack and rolled it on his wood. As he slid his fat head past her entry, she let out a deep gasp of pleasure. "Ooh yes, I like it Teco. Fuck me baby. Give it to me."

"Ooh you like that girl? Say fuck me."

"Fuck me; fuck me."

Lisa bit down on her lip as Teco drove into her. She was so wet; he put her on top of him. Her eyes told him that he was making all of the right moves. Lisa started calling his name out so loud that he put his hand over her mouth. He didn't want to disturb the people in the next room. Once she climaxed, he allowed himself to release also. They both lay there in bed breathing very heavy.

"Are you staying the night?" asked Lisa.

"Sure, let me call the front desk for a wake up call." Then they went back onto the balcony and smoked a joint.

◊◊◊◊◊

The next morning was the day that Teco and Lisa were called to testify. This was the first time Teco saw GQ in over two years. As Teco entered the courtroom, everyone was quiet.

"This is Case File Number FITEN01-HOM. I call Mr. Teco Jackson to take the stand," said D.A. Brown.

Teco looked at the white judge with pepper grey hair. Then he looked at GQ, who was staring at him with the evil look he had seen many times before. However, Teco still noticed that her eyes were stunning. He sat there trying to understand why GQ would hurt the man who cared for her the most.

"Will you raise your right hand and put your left hand on the bible? Do you swear to tell the truth, the whole truth, and nothing but the truth, so help you God?"

"I do," said Teco.

"You may be seated." Teco sat down and crossed his legs like a true gentleman. D.A. Brown asked Teco routine questions and turned to GQ's defense attorney and said, "Your witness, Attorney Butler."

Attorney Butler asked, "Are you on any prescription or illegal drugs that would prohibit you from telling the truth?"

"No."

"Will you state your full name please?"

"Teco Jackson."

"Do you have another name that people call you? If so, would you please tell the court?"

"Homicide."

"Are you a killer?"

"No sir."

"Why do they call you Homicide?"

"Because I was the enforcer for SB."

"What is SB?"

"A four crew team that sold drugs."

"Do you know Mujaheed Bashi Fiten?"

"Yes I do."

"Who is he?"

"He was the man who ran the crew."

"Didn't you have a reason to kill Mr. Fiten?"

"No I didn't."

"Didn't he leave you in jail?"

"Yes."

Teco started to fidget in his chair, because Attorney Butler was making it sound like Teco had something to do with Bashi's death.

"So you could have kill—"

D.A. Brown jumped to his feet, "I object your Honor. Defense is badgering the witness."

"Objection sustained."

"Are you or are you not wanted in Norristown?"

Teco looked at the judge and then D.A. Brown. "Not to my knowledge."

"Did you get arrested for carrying a sawed off pump shotgun in Norristown?"

"Your Honor objection to the question," said D.A. Brown.

"Your Honor, I will show motive and that Mr. Jackson is capable of killing Mr.—"

D.A. Brown and Attorney Butler started to argue. The judge slammed the gavel down three times. "Order in this courtroom. If this man is wanted, then he needs to be locked up."

"Your Honor, may I approach the bench?" asked D.A. Brown.

"Yes."

"Your Honor, here's Mr. Jackson's NCIC history."

The judge looked at the paperwork which D.A. Brown presented and said, "He is not wanted; and we'll take a 15 minute recess." Then he slammed the gavel down.

Teco was scared as hell and almost tripped as he came down from the witness stand. D.A. Brown said, "Teco, let me speak with you. Don't worry. I know that threw you off guard. I was prepared in case Attorney Butler tried that move. Therefore, I had the charges dropped. So don't worry."

After all testimonies and 5 hours of deliberation were over, the jury came in with the verdict.

The judge asked, "Will the defendant please rise? Madam Foreman, on the first count of the indictment, murder in the first degree, how do you find the defendant?"

"For docket number 85671, murder in the first degree, we the jury, for the Commonwealth of Philadelphia in the State of Pennsylvania, find the defendant, Gail Indigo Que, guilty."

People shouted and hugged each other.

"Order in the court," said the judge, who slammed the gavel down three times. The judge continued to say, "Ms. Que, what you did was brutal and crude. While you are in the penitentiary, you will have enough time to think about what you have done. I sentence you to

25 years to life for the murder of Mujaheed Bashi Fiten. This court is dismissed." Then the judge slammed the gavel down again.

GQ fainted. Attorney Butler shouted, "Get EMT in here right away!"

Bashi's family gave Teco hugs. Basil gripped Teco with a handshake that only they knew. Teco left the courthouse feeling that he had helped to put Bashi's killer behind bars for life. He went to D.A. Brown's building, where the secretary gave him a check for $1000. Teco walked down the hall to say thanks and goodbye. D.A. Brown said, "What's understood doesn't need to be explained." Then D.A. Brown and Teco exchanged firm handshakes.

Teco left the D.A.'s office. *"It's time for me to go back to D.C."* At the hotel, he had the front desk cash the check for him. Then he went to the 30th street station. This time there was no one looking for him.

On the Amtrak train, Teco was thinking about how he was going to change his life. A gorgeous dark-skinned young woman, who was dressed in a tailored grey and pink pinstripe suit, sat beside Teco. She smiled at him, but he didn't notice. When she cleared her throat, he looked into her radiant brown eyes. Without hesitation she said, "You look familiar. I went to a bridal shower not so long ago; and there was a dancer who looked just like you."

177

If you wish to contact the author, Kevin M. Weeks, the email address is *thestreetlifeseries@yahoo.com*. He looks forward to corresponding with you.

Printed in the United Kingdom
by Lightning Source UK Ltd.
117869UK00001B/151